A Step Beyond

Tales
By
Tom Herbert

DEDICATION

To my Father, Russell James Thomas Herbert, who always encouraged and supported me in my projects, and who gave rise to this work.

Tom Herbert: My story so far.

I began my first piece of creative writing around the age of nineteen. The theme was very surreal and rather ambitious, dealing with the profound effects the simple preparation of a cup of tea might have on other worlds and even universes (fictitious ones, of course).

Later, at the age of twenty-one, I wrote my first short story. It featured a businessman, travelling by sea, on his way home to England from an assignment somewhere in Europe. It could have been a very pleasant trip, but he spent most of it searching for a valuable pearl among the contents of a stuffed elephant that had somehow appeared in his cabin.

Although not usually quite so bizarre several of my stories contain a mysterious element. Others have comic, romantic, or religious content. Many feature ordinary people, often in less ordinary situations.

I have had a life-long interest in puppet theatre and joined the British Puppet & Model Theatre Guild in my late teens. Consequently, I have written several plays for this medium, including my Punch & Judy routine.

In my mid-twenties, I wrote my first (and so far only) full-length play for the live stage, a farcical comedy in three acts which, although I have since revised it, still requires some work.

More successfully, I have written several one-act plays for my local amateur dramatic society, The Woolgatherers of Heswall. They have always been very supportive of me and my work and have successfully performed two of my plays at the annual Heswall Arts Festival. Other plays are mainly short Christmas numbers that have also proved very popular.

After taking early retirement, I wrote my short story, *The Unfinished Shepherd,* which led me to become a member of Wirral Writers. Their encouragement and advice have been very important in the development of my writing, and it was during my time with them that I wrote most of my stories, including *The Apprentice,* which was short-listed in a competition run by Mags4Dorset in October 2011. I finally left after about eight years, not without regret, in order to devote more time to my other interests. I, however, hope to re-join soon.

It is still my ambition to write a novel, and I have made some headway into a fantasy novel, but it is far from complete. Unfortunately, as can often happen, more pressing pursuits and concerns have taken priority.

Having now amassed a quantity of my stories, I felt it was high time I did something with them. What use are they stuck on my laptop or as printed manuscripts in a plastic bag at the back of my wardrobe?

About a year before he died, my Father, Russell Herbert, said to me, "I want you to write something and get it published."

He was a hospital physicist in nuclear medicine and helped pioneer modern diagnostic scanning techniques from the 1950s to the early 1980s. At the time he said this, I was working at the Liverpool School of Tropical Medicine, and I thought he was hoping to see me write a scientific paper.

"No, not necessarily," he said. "It can be anything, anything at all."

So, here's to you, Dad. Some of my writing published a bit late in the day, perhaps.

I hope the reader will find something entertaining amongst these stories. As in the modern parlance – ENJOY!

Tom Herbert.

A STEP BEYOND - Tales by Tom Herbert

<u>ACKNOWLEDGEMENTS</u>

There are a number of people who have helped and supported me in producing this book, whether they realise it or not. My apologies to any that I may have left out.

Firstly, members of my family who have provided much-needed moral and practical support, including:

My Wife Linda Herbert, in particular, for proofreading the final text.
My Brother John Herbert; and
My Sister Ann Rivett.

In particular, I would like to thank my Niece Louise Rivett who designed and produced the cover for this book, as well as formatting my illustrations, patiently fielding all my persistent anxieties and bothers.

Also, my Sister-in-Law Anne Evans who advised me on the Welsh in my story *Fever or Forever*, and all other family members and friends who I know have been there in the background, willing me on.

Emma Hutt of The Word Hutt who has organised and undertaken all the practical work necessary for publication.

Staff and volunteers of the Wirral Society of the Blind & Partially Sighted, in particular Lynne Sedgewick, and Keith Ryan, who introduced me to Emma Hutt, and Kath Melling, who provided useful research information.

My thanks also go to Francesco Sorrentino, my mentor in all things Italian, who clarified a detail for me regarding Italy's language and culture in my story *Dutch Courage.*

Furthermore, I am indebted to:

Staff at the Liverpool Register Office.
Staff at the Libraries Archives of the Liverpool Record Office.
Staff at the British Newspaper Archive.
Staff at the Merseyside Maritime Museum.
All have readily provided useful advice and information for my research.

Tom Herbert

Life in Focus

THE WIDE BLUE YONDER

A hundred feet up, on a precipitous cliff edge, I jostled with my siblings as our mother brought us food, but I lost my footing and fell. Luckily the impact was broken by a clump of heather, and although initially stunned, I was not badly hurt. I was a week old and felt the clutches of hunger, along with the cold mountain air, beginning to grip. I cried out helplessly. It was not long before a dark shadow loomed over me. A predator! Was this the end?

Something grabbed me, and I was thrust into a dark, warm cavity. Whether I'd been eaten or not, I didn't know; but I felt more comfortable and began to settle down even with my gnawing hunger. There was an endless series of jolts and bumps; my captor seemed to be on the move. How long this went on for, I cannot say, but eventually, I was settled by my captor on a log in what looked like a dark cavern, being offered pieces of raw meat which I devoured hungrily.

The next day, sunshine came streaming in from an opening in the roof of my cell. The creature, which I later realised was a human, came in, offered me more meat, and continued to feed me at frequent intervals. After a few days, another human came with him to see me, and I heard them talking.

"It's a beautiful specimen, Clive. Where did you get it?"

"I found it at the bottom of a cliff as I was climbing near Snowdon. It must have fallen out of its nest. I'd like to rear it and train it to some jesses. I've always wanted a falcon."

"Clive, such raising of peregrines, particularly from the wild, is tightly controlled by law. It would be much better to raise it for release back from where it came."

"Yes, you're right."

Clive sounded disappointed but admitted, "I knew that working for the RSPB, you would give me some good advice."

"I'll do more than that. I'll come back tomorrow, put a ring on it, and we can rear it together."

The following day a ring was duly put on my leg. Although it felt a bit strange at first, it was light, loose-fitting, and gave me no trouble. I thrived, putting on weight. As I grew bigger, my down was gradually replaced by adult feathers. Every day, I exercised my wings, managing to raise myself from the ground with increasing ease.

One night, however, I heard creaking and cracking as someone I didn't recognise forced their way into my shelter. This human covered me with a black sack, tied it up, and took me away. I was taken to a dismal outhouse where I struggled to escape, but my captors held me fast and, none too gently, pulled off my ring. Later they tried to tempt me with what I now know were dead mice. These didn't look very appetising, but my hunger eventually got the better of me, and I ate one.

Early the next day, I was transferred to a wooden box and taken to a place where there was a lot of talking, booming and roaring. I was frightened; I had no idea what was happening, so I kept as still as possible. It wasn't long before I was moved to a place where there was a different noise, what I can only describe as a terrible whining sound. I didn't move a muscle, though I was getting hungry.

The air in my box was beginning to get rather stale and foetid. I needed to stretch my wings and my legs. In due course, my movements attracted attention.

"Here, what's in here?" said one voice.

"Equipment of some kind, I think," said another.

"We'd better have a look," said the first.

It was not without difficulty that they opened my box. The air was a bit fresher now, and I was being inspected by a couple of humans.

"A falcon, eh? Mm, it's got no ring. Illegal export! It's being smuggled. Take it back to the holding room. We must find out where it has come from."

So back I went. Time passed, and my attention was seized by several other voices, one of which I knew.

"It is illegal to export peregrines from Britain without full documentation. It should at least have a ring."

"It had one," said the voice I at once identified as my owner's. I blinked in the glare of some horrible artificial lights as I was taken out of my box and examined. The official continued talking to my owner.

"I also have photographs. See the markings on the breast, nape, and cheeks. They are exactly the same. And here in this close-up, you can see the ring and just about make out the number."

I was returned to my box, and there was a clicking sound.

"Are you sure it's here?" said the official.

"Yes," said my owner. I'm positive it's on this link." The clicking continued.

"Ah, yes, here it is."

"But there are no documents. It seems you were trying to smuggle it out of the country."

"I was doing no such thing," said Clive. "It was stolen from me. I guessed it might turn up here at the airport. I've come to take it back home. I'm rearing it for release into the wild. Here is my licence from Natural England. You can check with the RSPB if you like."

More clicking. Then the officer spoke again.

"Everything seems to be in order, sir. If you would just sign here, please. We'll need a photograph of the box, including its label and contents, so we can trace who is responsible."

There were bright flashes and more talking. Then Clive took me to his vehicle.

"Come on," he said. "You've had quite an adventure."

No sooner had I returned to the familiar shelter I called home than my strength seemed to leave me. I was no longer interested in food; I felt giddy and listless.

"What's the matter," said Clive. "You don't look well."

He tried to tempt me with various tit-bits but to no avail.

His friend came to visit me.

"I know a vet at the field station who specialises in raptors. We'll get her to have a look. Has it produced any pellets recently?"

"Just the one." Clive showed him.

"I see. Bring it with you. It may be useful in identifying the problem."

A human in overalls examined me carefully.

"What have you been feeding it?"

"Young chicks from a local farm."

"Anything else?"

Clive told her about me being stolen and how he had picked me up at the airport. The vet took the pellet and examined it carefully.

"It looks like it's had a mouse. Most likely one that has been eating poison. Try this in the bird's water. Use a syringe if necessary. Keep it warm and continue tempting it with delicacies. I'll see how it is in the next couple of days."

Clive nursed me very carefully, following the vet's instructions, and gradually my energy and strength returned.

"Well, Clive," said his friend one day. "It must be about five weeks old now. Time we introduced it to its true home. We'll have to camp out on the hillside. Are you up for it?"

"I'll be sorry to see it go, but yes, that is where it belongs. How about next week?"

"Where are they taking me?" I wondered. "Surely, this is my home?"

I had completely forgotten my eyrie on the cliff. After a long, bumpy journey, I looked out over a wide landscape of mountains and moorland. The chilly wind ruffled my feathers, and I wished I was back in my comfortable shelter.

"This is about where I found it. We can pitch over here," said Clive.

In the shelter of a large rock, my humans raised a kind of refuge. Clive's friend pointed to the sky.

"Look! There are a couple of young peregrines up there about the same age as this one."

"Do you think they're its siblings?"

"Possibly. See them teasing that raven. A bit ambitious, I think. Why don't we let this one go and see what it does?"

They opened my basket and helped me out. I stretched out my wings. The air was exhilarating, and I felt the wind buoy me up. Soon I was airborne, and I joined the other two in the sky. We had a wonderful time, reaching for each other's tails in mock strikes. I thrilled with the sensation of wheeling and soaring over the rugged landscape, but hunger eventually forced me back to my humans, and I spent the night on a rock outside their refuge.

I was still fed morsels of meat, but not enough to satisfy me. Every day I joined my peers in their games of tag in the air, but my food rations became smaller and less frequent, increasing my hunger, until one day, they stopped altogether. About that time, one of the parent birds flew over carrying a live plover which it dropped.

Immediately one of the youngsters swooped on it and bore it off to a rock, where it proceeded to tear the bird apart and devour the soft, warm flesh. How succulent it looked. How satisfying. I was envious, and my hunger increased. Later that day, in the same way, one of the adults brought a ring ouzel, but although I made a valiant attempt to catch it, one of the others got there first. I was determined not to miss the next chance.

I spent another hungry night near the humans' refuge, wishing they would feed me. Early the next morning, I returned to the air, my senses heightened and ready. Soon one of the parent birds appeared with a curlew still struggling, which it dropped. I needed no prompting and immediately dived on the prey and made my first kill. Breakfast had never tasted so good.

I became more adept at catching these offerings until, still dogged by hunger, I decided to try and catch something for myself. I had often seen the adult birds hunting, and having now had some practice catching prey, I made several stoops on likely-looking victims. I was amazed how they sensed my presence long before I reached them. I knew I must not give up. If others could do it, so could I. Sailing high up in the sky, I spied a flock of meadow pipits. I began my dive, twisting, and pumping my wings to increase my velocity, then pressed them close to my body to become more streamlined. Faster and faster, I raced, thrusting out my talons as I reached that flock of birds. They all scattered in wild alarm, and no one was more surprised than me to find

I'd got one. It barely made a snack, but I was the proudest falcon in Snowdonia.

Perfecting my technique took time and practice, but eventually, I became a skilled hunter. I spent more and more time soaring over snowy mountains and green valleys out in the wide blue yonder. The humans that had reared me so carefully had packed up their refuge several days before, returning back down the hillside.

"That's a good job done, Clive. I doubt if he'll be needing us anymore, but why don't we come back in a month or so just to see what's going on."

I was free. Free to be the master of this vast and wonderful wilderness. My home.

DUTCH COURAGE

A lion's growl filtered through the murk as Chico picked his way between the trailers. He had now got his bearings. He was near Ivan's cage and could just about make out a large shape pacing up and down in a trailer, bordered by a façade, cut and painted to make it look like a cave.

The audience had been well down in numbers that night but had made up for it in their animated response to his antics. Fog like this occasionally occurred in the region, said by the experts to be caused partly by local volcanic activity. It was oppressive, so making people laugh was difficult. However, it had been a good show despite the weather.

Chico gave a start as a bushy head came into view. It was Mario with a bucket of meat and an unsteady gait.

"Good show tonight, Chico," he said, slapping him on the back.

"Thank you, Mario; they loved your act with Ivan too. But I wish you wouldn't drink before going on."

"Just a drop for courage, my friend. I couldn't work without it. Ha, what's this?"

He picked up something from the ground and put it with the food.

"Ivan nearly lost part of his dinner. It must have fallen out. He won't be happy with short rations."

La Meraviglia was a small circus that toured Puglia and the surrounding countryside in southern Italy. Its members lived a frugal existence, and that the business survived at all was indeed a marvel. Shopping amongst the market stalls, he looked like any other pensioner, but to this little company of performers, Chico was their chief and only clown. Although his age was catching up with him, and he could no longer tumble as he used to, he could still hold an audience with his jokes, tricks, and buffoonery.

At last, Chico reached his caravan, and a friendly glow soon pierced the gloom as he lit his oil lamp. He sat down and checked his props bag. Inside was a slap stick, a wilting flower, a horn on a rubber bulb, a whistle, and a gun that displayed a flag with BANG! written on it; a string of sausages, and, oh! Where was the rubber chicken?

"It must be here somewhere", he said to himself, tipping the contents on the bed. "Perhaps I've left it in the Big Top."

Then an awful thought occurred to him. What if it had fallen out when he bumped into Mario, and that was the object he had picked up, too drunk to realise what it was? The terrible consequences did not bear thinking of. Even on a purely practical level, the vet's bill would be unaffordable; also, the loss of their one and only lion would mean a severe drop in the takings. Apart from this, Ivan was a circus favourite; the idea of him suffering because of his carelessness was too much for Chico to contemplate. He returned to the lion's cave with a flashlight and scanned inside the trailer. Ivan was resting after his meal. His eyes shone as he blinked in the torch beam, but he did not seem inclined to get up.

"I hope he hasn't got bellyache", Chico thought with mounting consternation.

He searched amongst the bedding. There was the odd bone; and a pile of dung, its rank smell lingering in the fog. He examined every nook and cranny as far as the shadows allowed him and was about to give up when he saw something poking out from under the straw. It was the head of his rubber chicken, but his anxiety increased.

"Supposing that's all there is of it. Whatever shall I do? How can I retrieve it?"

Chico decided the first thing to do was to see Mario. The lion tamer warmly invited the clown into his rather cramped quarters, cluttered with circus memorabilia.

"Chico, my dear friend. How good of you to call. Come and join me in a bottle of wine."

"Mario, this isn't a social visit. I'm in a bit of a pickle, and I need your help."

He told him about the mix-up with the rubber chicken, but he only laughed.

"Don't worry; we'll deal with it in the morning. Have a drop of courage. I don't know why you don't use a real chicken. It would save all this trouble."

"That's ridiculous, and you know it. For a start, think of the expense and the mess it would make of my sausage machine."

Mario paid no attention to him. He was drunk and not in any condition to understand, let alone help. At least he was quite happy to let him borrow his old coat and the keys to the lion's cave.

Chico asked other circus members, including Paolo, the tight rope walker and Carlo, the acrobat, but he couldn't persuade them to help him. He was a clown. They thought it all very funny and would not take him seriously. Daffodil was the one exception. She was a student from the Netherlands who had joined the circus during her gap year and had stayed on ever since. She was a slight little thing who wore sequined costumes and colourful feathered headdresses while performing tricks on horseback. Having overheard Chico explaining his problem to Giacomo, the fire-eater, she offered to help.

"But Daffodil, what can you do? How could you help if Ivan turned nasty? It's too dangerous. I could never allow you to put yourself at such risk."

"Oh, Chico, you are very sweet, but I am not such a delicate flower as you may think. At least I have a strong voice and can get help if necessary."

Daffodil went back with Chico to his caravan, where she watched him don a big black curly wig and a shaggy black beard. He then put on Mario's old coat to complete his disguise.

"There, what do you think?"

"You don't look much like Mario to me", she laughed, "but then I'm not Ivan. Poo! That coat stinks!"

"It's the one Mario uses when he cleans out Ivan's cave and feeds him. There's one more important thing."

He took a big steak from his cold box and gazed at it lovingly.

"This was a gift from a delighted spectator. I was so looking forward to this for my supper, but now I suppose I will have to sacrifice it to get my rubber chicken back."

"Not a very good exchange", said Daffodil, "but necessary, I suppose."

There was no way Chico could dissuade Daffodil from coming with him, so he gave her a broom in case of trouble and told her to keep watch at the front of the trailer. Slowly, and fearfully he unlocked the door at the rear. He heard the lion stand up with a growl and Daffodil coaxing him to the end of his cave, distracting him with the steak. Chico crept in as quietly as he could through the dry straw. Now, where was it? Everything looked very different from the other side, so locating the chicken seemed to take him an age. Then came the dangerous part, bending down. His arthritis was such a problem. While he picked up the rubber chicken, Daffodil fed Ivan the steak. It had looked like a really big steak, but in his huge mouth, it was only a morsel.

"Look out, Chico!" she said.

He froze as the lion came toward him. Although Chico had closed the door, he had not secured it properly so that, if necessary, he could make a quick escape, but the great beast turned to the back of the cave and barred the exit. The old man was trying to summon up the courage to approach it when to his horror, with a flick of his paw, Ivan managed to open the door and was free. With much trepidation, Chico followed the animal out into the foggy night. He could hear Daffodil calling softly,

"Ivan, Ivan."

What chance had they of finding him in these conditions? Ranging about with his torch, he caught the glint of two eyes only a few feet from him.

"Move away from the door," he heard Daffodil say calmly.

He did so, gingerly edging himself down the side of the trailer. At that moment, the silence was broken by loud shouts of, "Hoa! Hoa!"

The svelte little Dutch girl burst into view and rushed at the lion while beating the ground with the broom. Without further persuasion, Ivan decided his cage was preferable to freedom and bounded back inside, at which point Chico quickly shut the door and locked it.

They both stood in the fog, gasping with relief. On examination, the chicken had a few tears, but by and large, it was intact. Apparently, Ivan hadn't thought much of it and had rejected it with great disdain. As far as he was concerned, it bore no resemblance to anything he liked to eat.

"So it's rubber chicken for supper tonight, Chico?"

"I've got a couple of eggs", he murmured.

"That steak was no small sacrifice. Why don't you join me?"

Chico gratefully accepted.

"I admire your courage. I would never have...."

"It's nothing." Daffodil shrugged. "I hope you like chicken stew, but please, leave that coat behind."

At that, they both dissolved into helpless laughter.

SAVING FACE

For centuries, the old bridge had survived every onslaught from man and nature alike. It had always been there and was even mentioned in the Domesday Book. Popular with tourists, photographs of it must grace half the albums in the world. Generations of children had caught fish from it, and ducks had raised their broods in its shadow. Small wonder its collapse caused no little stir in the nearby village.

"As the damage is so serious," said Councillor Hawksley, "is it worth repairing? It would be cheaper to demolish the bridge and build a copy. Tourists would be none the wiser."

"We can't possibly do that," said Nellie Pickles. "It would be very dishonest to our visitors. Just think of the scandal and the damage to our trade when – I'm not saying if, but when – the truth leaks out. So we must make every effort to repair it."

Nods and grunts of approval went around the room. Then, Mildred Potter, the librarian, spoke up.

"What about the face?"

"What face?" said Mervin Brook, the headmaster.

"The Green Man," replied Mildred, "in the middle of the parapet overlooking the river. It dates back to Saxon times and has always been part of the bridge."

The Councillor gave a weary sigh. "Hardly a good enough reason to restore it. Let us move on."

They continued with the agenda until 'Any Other Business' when Mildred spoke once more.

"There is a legend that says if the face were to leave the bridge, the village would fall into ruin."

"I think I've heard something to that effect, too," said Nellie, though she wasn't at all sure if she had.

"Complete and utter rubbish," said Mervin. "I'm not wasting my time arguing about fairy tales," and walked out, followed by a large percentage of the committee.

Nellie and Mildred drew up a poster featuring a big question mark reading, "Do you care about our village? Meeting above The Cock and Bull next Wednesday at 7-30pm."

The attendance was better than they had hoped.

"I will not be a party to any superstition," said Amos Barford the Vicar, "but I feel the bridge is a great treasure."

All agreed that it should be restored.

"Do we know where the face is?" asked Ethel, who ran the gift shop. "And is it still intact?"

"Good question," said Mildred. "We will look into it and report back as soon as possible."

Dressed for action in her Wellington boots, Mildred met Nellie at the bridge.

"I'm going in for a good look," she said and waded out into the river.

"Oh, do be careful," said Nellie.

"Come on," her friend insisted.

Nellie squealed as the chilly water grasped her feet.

"Don't be such a wimp," urged Mildred impatiently.

Searching the rubble, she found the stone that had held the Green Man, but the entire face was missing.

"Are you sure it's the right stone?" asked Nellie.

"Of course I am. Look, you can see where it has been."

Nellie examined the area carefully with a magnifying glass

"Someone's chiselled it off," she said, indicating some abrasions.

"No, they haven't. The original Saxon stone masons made those marks. They look fresh because they've always been covered up."

Nellie stared in amazement.

Mildred persisted. "It must be somewhere here in the river."

At that moment, she gave a yell as she lost her footing on the wet rocks. Nellie tried to help her up but in vain.

"Get help," Mildred ordered. "I think I've twisted my ankle."

"Yes, of course," said Nellie in a dither. "Stay there."

That evening they sat in Mildred's lounge, consoling each other with hot chocolate. Braced and bandaged, Mildred nursed her ankle swathed in a sheepskin rug by the fire as they discussed what to do.

"We must save the Green Man," Mildred insisted.

Nellie agreed. If Mildred's injury was the beginning of the bad luck, what would happen next?

"There's not much I can do like this," she said. "You must get some assistance. I'll have to direct operations from here."

"Alright, dear," said Nellie. "I'll do what I can."

How did Mildred always manage to evade the hard work?

"You mark my words; unpleasant things will happen," said Mildred to Nellie. "The Easter Fayre is coming up, and the vicar is hoping to raise enough money to kick-start repairs to the church roof, but I'll be surprised if he is successful."

Just as Mildred predicted, the fayre's takings were well down on previous years.

"There's barely enough to buy new hymn books, ancient or modern," she said. "We need more help. People must be reminded that things are going from bad to worse in this village. See if you can book the Women's Institute for another meeting."

Mildred displayed a photograph of the Green Man. A leafy face in stone.

"Don't you think this is going too far?" said Alice, the hairdresser. "I mean, when all's said and done, it's only a bit of rock."

She was suspicious that Mildred had a hidden agenda.

A bleak gloom settled over the village until one day in late summer, some builders appeared at the bridge and began the task of restoring it. At the next committee meeting, Councillor Hawksley announced that an American, falling in love with the village after several visits, had donated funds specifically to repair the bridge and the church roof.

"The only problem is," said the Councillor, "There is a proviso that the Green Man must be returned to its original place on the bridge, and unfortunately, it appears to be lost."

At that point, Mildred stood up very proudly and said that after much searching, she had finally found it. Greatly relieved, the whole committee applauded and congratulated her.

Everyone in the village became noticeably happier, walking with more of a spring in their step. Everyone, that is, except Mildred herself. She had a dark secret. Determined to improve her prestige in the community, the collapse of the bridge had provided her with the opportunity to do just that. An amateur archaeologist, Mildred had expertly chiselled the face from its setting and fabricating the legend had planned to bring out the Green Man at a favourable moment, to great acclaim. Now, however, counter to the resulting jubilation, she was in the depths of despair. The face, which she had hidden in her broom cupboard, to her horror, had gone. As the bridge neared completion, Mildred's anxieties increased. To make matters worse, some people made fun of her, saying how foolish she was to believe in the superstition, especially now that the repairs were almost finished. After yet another sleepless night, unable to bear it any longer, Mildred decided to confide in her friend, Nellie. Over tea and Madeira cake, she poured out the whole sorry tale.

"What shall I do? I will never be able to show my face in the village again," she wailed.

Relishing having the upper hand for once, Nellie was almost overbearing with her sympathy. Mildred felt the cake crumble in her hand, crumbs dropping on the carpet. Mortified, she insisted on clearing them up and sweeping aside her protests; she forged ahead to Nellie's broom cupboard, opened the door, and stood dumbfounded.

"Oh! Do my eyes deceive me?" she cried, for there, staring back at her, lay the Green Man.

Now it was Nellie's turn to confess. While looking for the bathroom during one of her visits to Mildred, she had accidentally opened the broom cupboard door. Speechless at what she saw and tired of playing second fiddle, she had taken advantage of Mildred's incapacity in order to appropriate the Green Man.

"There's only one way for us to save face," counselled Nellie. "We must present it to the committee together, saying we both found it. After all, it is the truth. In a way." Reluctantly, Mildred agreed.

At a ceremony to mark the completion of the bridge, Councillor Hawksley commended Mildred and Nellie for finding the Green Man.

"We are indebted to you both," he said, unveiling a plaque, to the fact, in their honour. "Without your sterling work, this renovation would not have been possible."

"Ladies!" gushed the Reverend Barford. "Alice has suggested you write an account for the church newsletter about how you found the Green Man."

"An interview, please." asked a reporter.

The two women looked at each other and swallowed hard.

"I think we can come up with something," said Mildred.

"Er, yes, of course," Nellie concurred rather hesitantly.

Alice smiled sweetly.

"People would be most fascinated," she assured them.

THE PRIZE

"It couldn't have happened to a nicer man," said Mrs Doyle. She'd come to the post office to buy a book of first-class stamps,

"Oh, the price of postage these days," said Phyllis Peek. "You might as well buy a train ticket and take the letters yourself."

"Arthur would never agree to me gallivanting off all the time like that. He'd starve to death. Mind you; he could do with losing a few pounds."

"I was only joking, Maggie, but who is this you're talking about?"

"Oh yes. As I said, it couldn't have happened to a nicer man. That Mr Phillips, he's really good-hearted, do anything for anyone."

Phyllis was getting a bit impatient. She wanted to hear the juicy bit. Everyone knew Mr Phillips was a pillar of the community. He was always helping to raise money for some good cause or other or getting stuck into some building project. He was an excellent organiser. Very seldom did he take a holiday and certainly wouldn't dream of taking any profits for himself.

"Come on, Maggie, don't keep me hanging on. I've got to meet our Billy at the school in half an hour."

"Where was I?"

Mrs Doyle was easily side-tracked, and her memory was a bit suspect, but she always knew the latest gossip.

"You know very well. You said it couldn't happen to a nicer man."

"Oh yes, Mr Phillips. He went in for this competition, you see. Had to say why he liked foreign holidays in no more than a hundred words."

Phyllis exclaimed that he'd never been on a foreign holiday to her knowledge, so how could he know anything about them? Maggie explained that it was run by Paradise Tours, and the prize was a holiday for two on a Caribbean cruise.

"Well, Phyllis, of course, he won, didn't he?"

"But he's a widower; he lives on his own. Who is he going to take with him?"

This is what everyone was talking about. People were queuing up to go with him or at least trying to persuade him to raffle the prize so that they all had a chance to go.

"But Maggie, those things are usually non-transferable."

"You could be right, Phyllis, but do you really think Paradise Holidays are going to check up on his identity? Anyone could say they're him, couldn't they?"

"I'm not so sure, Maggie. Sorry, I must go, or I'll be late to meet Billy."

Brian Phillips had lost count of the times he'd put the phone down, saying, "I'll make my decision in due course. Until then, you'll have to wait like everybody else."

It was getting so annoying that he finally recorded it on his answering machine.

What was he to do about all his projects and interests while he was gone? For a start, there was nobody else to take over the fund for building the new church hall. Or to organise the pensioners' supper. What was he to do about the scouts' camp or the school open day, particularly as he was on the board of governors? He didn't even have a television because he was so busy writing letters, attending meetings, and organising any number of events.

The day came while he was going to a charity fair that he was expected to open. Unfortunately, the train had stopped beside an industrial waste ground. The waiting seemed interminable as he gazed through rain-spattered windows until, at last, a voice came over the intercom.

"This train for Crewe will be delayed for approximately one hour; we are very sorry for the inconvenience."

Very sorry, very sorry. That was no good; he had an important deadline to keep. He managed to waylay a ticket official and explained how important this appointment was.

"Unfortunately, sir. Everyone's in the same boat, or should I say train? My little joke."

Little joke, this was important. People were relying on him. What would happen if he didn't turn up on time, worse still, not at all? He had taken the train to avoid delays due to road works, and now here he was, stuck in the middle of nowhere. Not turning up to this event would be bad enough, but he had also promised to attend a parish council meeting that evening.

"I'm afraid there's a blockage on the line ahead, sir. We must wait until it's been cleared. A tree has come down, I think."

Mr Phillips felt in his pockets. How could he possibly have forgotten his mobile phone? In an effort to cut down on unnecessary baggage, he'd left his laptop at home, intending to use his mobile if he had to get in touch with people. How could he have been so foolish? He looked in his briefcase, which smelled of new leather, finally taking out a recent edition of Readers Digest. He scanned the pages looking for something of interest and started reading an article on the perils of journeying to Madagascar in an effort to distract himself, but he couldn't really settle on anything. He sat looking out at the dismal scene watching a couple of crows squabbling over a find on a large rubbish tip. His muscles were tightening; his hands were cold and clammy; he felt dizzy and rather nauseous. Oh, how he wished the train would get a move on. The intercom came on again.

"We regret the continuing delay, ladies and gentlemen, but we are still waiting for the experts to clear the tree from the line. We apologise for any inconvenience."

Hadn't they even started yet? Brian was under the impression that they were at least halfway through. He wondered if he should get out and help somehow, but there didn't seem to be any future in it. His brain felt numb. He tried to relax, perhaps have a little nap, but all the time, he felt as though he was trying to keep a lid on a volcano about to erupt. The pressure was building up all the time until his eyes began to leak, but there was no relief. What was happening? Was he going to explode? Noises like choking came from him. People began to turn and look. The choking became louder and more violent until the dam burst, and he broke down into uncontrollable wailing, sobbing, and blubbering. Mr Phillips' embarrassment was extreme, which only made things worse, and there was nothing he could do about it.

Brian's memory of returning home was little more than a blur. However, the charity fair and the parish council meeting seemed to have managed quite well without him. Now he was seated, pouring out his soul before a woman he didn't even know. He explained about the holiday he had won and the problem of who was to go with him. Where were all his negotiation and logistic skills now?

"Just the thing, Mr Phillips," he heard the counsellor say. "I suggest you take that cruise with both hands and leave all your worries behind. All you have to do is to decide who you are going to take with you."

Brian thought for a while. Who was there? Hundreds of people seemed to be clamouring for the chance to come with him, but where were his friends? Life seemed to have passed him by.

"You don't have to make up your mind right now, Mr Phillips. There's no hurry. Mull it over for a while."

For the first time, here was a woman more interested in him than anything he had to offer. Now, where was that genius for making snap decisions he was so well known for? The silence was deafening.

"I've decided," said Brian after what seemed an eternity. "I would like you to come with me."

THE BULL

Beth missed her sister. Oh, they had their quarrels and arguments as all siblings do, but they had good times together too. Now Hannah was living miles away with her husband and newborn baby, and Beth was left alone with her parents.

Her sister's marriage, by all accounts, was a very happy one, and Beth wished she too could find Mr Right. Academically, she was a bright girl and was studying for her A levels, but recently social media was intruding, and she spent more time with it than she should.

One evening, when her parents thought she was writing an essay, a friend request appeared from a young man who just called himself The Bull. This should have rung warning bells immediately, but Beth was intrigued. From his photograph, he was very good looking, not much older than herself, and with similar interests. During the weeks that followed, she spent more and more time chatting with him over the internet. There finally came the point when he looked for a closer relationship.

"You and I were made for each other," he said. "I'd love to meet you."

Her heart gave a little jump. A boyfriend at last. Could he be the one?

"Meet me at the Hog's Head in Melton Street next Saturday at eight pm," he texted. "But don't tell anyone. It will be our secret. Can't wait."

She didn't know where this place was but was sure she could find out easily enough. Beth could hardly contain herself during the next few days and eventually told her secret to a friend at college.

"Oh, Beth, you're mad. It's terribly dangerous."

Beth was too excited to listen to reason. Her friend tried to telephone her parents to warn them of their daughter's intentions. After trying several times, she finally got an answer.

"I'm not sure where she's going, but you've got to stop her."

Unfortunately, it was too late. Beth had already gone. Melton Street was a poorly lit side road in a run-down part of town she had never been in before. Nervously, she walked into the bar, looking around her, checking her watch, and a photograph in her hand. After about ten minutes, she wondered if she had made a mistake, then she gave a start as a heavy hand landed on her shoulder.

"Hello Beth," said a deep voice.

She turned to see a heavily built man over twice her age. He had untidy black hair and dark stubble on his chin.

"Glad you could make it."

"Who are you? I'm meeting someone here."

"I am The Bull, and you're coming with me."

"No, no, you can't be."

She struggled to get away from him and was about to shout for help when he clamped his hand over her mouth and hustled her out into the dark street. No one in the bar seemed to take any notice, as though they had seen it all before. He tied her hands behind her back, put a gag around her mouth, blindfolded her, bundled her into a car, and drove off. Now she wished she had listened to her inner voice and warnings from her friend. What would happen to her? Her heart beat like a trapped bird, and she wished she were back home, a prospect which was beginning to seem increasingly unlikely.

How long they drove for, she couldn't tell. Two hours perhaps? Neither had she any idea where she was being taken. Eventually, the car pulled up at a front door in a lonely street. The Bull opened it, dragged her out, and pushed her into the building, locking the door behind him.

She stumbled up the stairs, and The Bull thrust her to the floor. Roughly he untied her and removed the scarf from her eyes. She was in a dingy room with paper peeling from the damp walls. The only item of furniture was the bed against which she was pushed. Shaking with fear, Beth implored him not to hurt her. The Bull grunted.

"Give me your phone," he said.

"I, I haven't got one."

"Liar!" he said, smacking her across the face.

He looked in her clutch bag and not finding one manhandled her until he found it in an inside pocket of her jacket. She fought and kicked but was no match for him.

"You'll do as you're told if you know what's good for you," said The Bull and left the room, locking the door behind him.

She searched for some means of escape. Sheets of plywood covered the windows, making the room dark and airless. She kicked and hammered at the door, desperately turning and rattling the handle in a vain attempt to escape. Beth slumped to the floor in uncontrollable sobs. What was the use? It was impossible.

She began to pray, something she hadn't done since childhood, and after about an hour, she heard footsteps on the stairs. More than one person, it seemed. The Bull came in with a swarthy companion in a dirty raincoat.

"Here she is. What do you think of her? Nice little catch, isn't she?"

"Depends if she can do the business," said the other. "How much do you want for her?"

Her captor gave him a price.

"What! She's not worth that. I can get one like her any day," and he offered half the price.

The bartering became more and more acrimonious.

"Don't try to swindle me," said the man in the raincoat.

"Why should I be beaten down by the likes of you? She cost me a lot of time and effort, not to mention petrol."

Becoming increasingly irate, The Bull pulled a gun from his pocket.

"Don't play games with me."

The other one tried to talk him down, and after some coaxing, The Bull responded just enough for the man in the raincoat to draw his own weapon. Slowly they circled, glaring at each other. After a stand-off that seemed to go on forever, one of them jerked his hand as if he was about to shoot. The other fired seconds before his adversary. Beth screamed. The two men lurched and fell to the floor. They lay there motionless, blood oozing from their chests. Beth moved cautiously. Neither of the men stirred. One of them had fallen heavily with his head against the door. It would be difficult to open. She turned the handle and pulled the door hard, opening it just enough to squeeze out. As she pushed her way through, a hand grabbed her ankle.

"Not so fast," said The Bull."

"Let me go, let me go," yelled Beth, kicking him violently.

Certainly, he was not dead, but being weakened, his grip was not as tight as it had been. Beth managed to pull herself away and fled out of the house, leaving her shoe in The Bull's grasp.

LOVE'S STING

In a club behind Liverpool's Lime Street Station, Sean Sullivan, his mind elsewhere, mechanically served drinks to animated customers. Everyone knew him as Xavier. It sounded cool, unlike his own boring name. Being barman in the Fanfare Club on a Friday night was no fun, but it paid the bills; just. He hankered after fame and affluence as an entertainer. His latest song, Hermosa's Hacienda, was about an adventurer searching for a girl in Mexico. He dreamed of setting out by himself, with his guitar, but since his fiasco, in Italy, he didn't have the nerve. A job on a cruise ship might provide some opportunities, but what if he didn't like it?

The Honey Pot Cafe was closing, and Sandra Kennelly had replaced her starched apron with her faux fur coat.

"Come on, Sand."

Marni poked her redhead around the rather shabby service door.

"We're not letting you go like this."

The rest of the staff followed her inside.

"A little bird told us today's your birthday, so we're taking you out to the Fanfare Club tonight."

"Sorry girls, I'm babysitting for our Bella."

"But, Sand, it's your birthday. Tell your daughter you're coming with us, and we won't take no for an answer."

Sandra knew they meant it, and why shouldn't she go out for her birthday?

"But Mum, I promised to visit some customers tonight."

"Can't Dean mind, Jamie?"

"You're joking! My brother?"

"It is my birthday, you know."

"Oh God, Mum, I'm sorry. I forgot. I'll ask Donna to do it. You go and enjoy yourself."

The girls commandeered a table near the bar, the D. J. played golden oldies, and drink was beginning to flow.

"Snowball, OK for you, Sand?"

"Thanks, Cheryl. Hey, Waterloo. I love this one. Let's have a jig."

Several got up and began to boogie while the others watched the handbags.

"I say, Sand; that barman's pretty hot".

"He might suit you, Mel, but I'm old enough to be his mother."

The music died down, and the D.J. stood up.

"We have a birthday celebration tonight. So come out, Sandra Kennelly."

He presented her with a small cake crowned with a single candle.

"Twenty-one again, love. Now blow it out and make a wish."

She wished she was babysitting.

"Give her a big hand, everyone."

Marni calculated on her fingers.

"I reckon that barman must be about thirty. If he was your kid, you would have been about eighteen when he was born."

Sandra flushed, "It was only a joke, Marn."

"We wanna know all about it," chimed in the others.

More drinks were ordered, hoping they might loosen her up, but Sandra would not be drawn.

An unfamiliar bluesy number was played next, sung in a husky male voice.

"Love's Sting," announced the D.J. "By our very own Xavier, who will play a few more for you tonight."

Sean appeared with his guitar and sporting a black leather jacket. He'd worn it at some of his, occasionally, more successful gigs leading him to regard it as lucky.

His audience gave a rather languid clap.

"Thank you, ladies and gentlemen. Those were from my latest album, Steamy Kitch, available now from the bar."

It was, in fact, his only album, produced in a seedy studio off Bold Street.

"Sandie, I never expected to see you here," said a woman about her own age. "Where have you been? Some of the girls from the travel agency are having a little reunion. We've kept in touch since it closed. They all remember you. Come and join us?"

"Sorry, Mag. These friends have brought me here for my birthday."

"Bring them over here?" said Marni quickly.

She was hoping they might help Sandra divulge some of her affairs.

The table was expanded into two; cocktails were brought, and one of the new arrivals asked Sandra how her children were.

She told her about Bella and her job as a cosmetics representative and Dean's problems with his website.

"What about your other one?" asked a lady wearing a spicy scent redolent of the 1970s.

"Lovely little lad he was. Such a shame."

"Ah aye, what happened, Sand?" asked Mel.

"I was young and daft. Fell for the first man I fancied."

"You didn't marry him, did you?"

"I had to. I was pregnant. Our parents insisted. I thought we'd be happy; we were for a few months, but he became increasingly abusive after the baby was born. He accused me of having affairs until, eventually, I did. The divorce was very messy. He told a lot of lies to get custody of our child. We called him Sean. I haven't seen him since he was four years old."

Tearful, Sandra's voice was breaking as she filled a hopelessly small tissue.

"He disappeared, of course, Soon after."

"You know, Sand? There's just a chance our singing barman is your child."

"Come off it, Marni! Xavier?"

"I've heard others behind the bar call him Sean, and he's about the right age."

"I've more chance of winning the lottery. Anyway, he's probably changed his surname."

One of the travel brigade added,

"Sullivan, wasn't it?"

"Thanks, Win, I do know," retorted Sandra, armed with a fresh tissue.

At the bar, Marni looked for traces of Sandra in the barman's face.

"Yes, love?"

"Er, a gin and tonic, please, Mr, er."

"Just Xavier."

"Could I ask you a personal question?"

"You from the press?"

Marni thought for a second. That was an idea.

"Not exactly. I'm a talent scout."

Perhaps the jacket was lucky after all. Sotto voce, he answered, "I finish soon. The name's Sean Sullivan. Here's my card."

Marni returned with some haste.

"Well, Sand, his surname is Sullivan."

Mag put in her two-penny-worth.

"There must be loads of Sean Sullivans around."

Marni, however, pursued the matter.

"Did you give him a middle name, Sand?"

"No, but I did give him a pet name just between him and me."

"C'mon. Tell us. What was it?"

After what seemed an age, the name escaped from Sandra's lips.

"Pigly."

That had to be the clincher. Ostensibly about to order more drinks, Marni called, "Hey, Pigly!"

Xavier spun round galvanised as if by an electric shock, then stood immobile for a moment, open-mouthed.

"Where did you get that name from?"

Marnie grinned and just said, "Your mother wants you."

THE APPRENTICE

The remote Alpine town in which this story is set has always been difficult to reach, and even today, it is best approached by a four-wheel-drive vehicle. The town is dominated by a modest castle, which has been the seat of the community's affairs for centuries. Here, a large clock, not quite as old as the castle itself, has pride of place facing the square, and each hour, the figure of a blacksmith raises his hammer and strikes a sonorous anvil.

TSH

In the highest turret is an observatory from where the celestial spheres may be studied. This is the residence and workplace of the town's Time Master, who maintains the big clock and ensures it is accurate so that the townsfolk can go about their daily affairs in an orderly, harmonious fashion.

Before the age of radio and television, this was the only way people could set their timepieces. In those days, there was a Time Master named Ardit. He was a thin, wizened little man with a beak-like nose, and thinning, untidy hair. Ardit could tell the precise hour by studying the heavens. If the clock ever erred one way or another, he would alter the weights to bring it back to perfect time. His job was also to clean and oil the mechanism, replacing worn parts if necessary. He was the only person in the town who had this knowledge, and as a great deal of learning and understanding was required, he was held in great respect by the townsfolk, almost as if he were a magician.

Nevertheless, Ardit realised that sooner or later, someone would have to take over from him, so he appointed an apprentice from the youth of the town. He chose a boy named Serge, who showed no little aptitude in all aspects of the work, the science and its practical applications. Feeling he had found the ideal person, he set himself to teach his apprentice all he knew. Serge learnt quickly, but only after many months and under careful supervision did the Time Master allow him to attempt any of the more important duties.

Several years into his training, Serge noticed that the clock was beginning to lose time and had to be adjusted more frequently. He informed the Time Master of this, and they discovered that one of the parts was worn, which, if not replaced, would eventually cause the clock to stop altogether. Although there were two skilled horologists in the community, neither could supply such a large and specialised part. The only person Ardit knew who could make it lived in the neighbouring town, some miles away, over rough terrain.

Many days were spent making measurements and drawing accurate plans. When they were complete, Ardit set the clock so that only the basic attention was necessary while he was away. He gave Serge strict instructions on making minor daily adjustments by adding or subtracting a few coins each day to the weights according to the calculations he had taught him. Finally, the Time Master prepared his mules for the journey and left.

Serge was very conscientious, and for a while, all went well; but it was a lonely job in the castle tower, and when the time came for him to finish his day's work, he was more than happy to relax in a bar with some friends. Like most folk in the town, he enjoyed a game of Jass and was quite adept at this card game. One night, after several mugs of the strong, local brew, being over-confident, he bet a month's wages. It was only when he woke the following day that he realised, to his horror, the money that he owed.

Back at his post, the coins for regulating the clock became more and more tempting.

"Surely", he thought, "any piece of metal would do."

So he went to the local blacksmith to scrounge old washers to replace the coins. Everything continued as normal; the people were regulating their clocks as usual. Soon, however, they noticed that the sun began to rise and set at times quite out of keeping with the season, and the livestock needed feeding or milking at unusual hours. Routines and appointments also seemed to go awry. Slowly, people realised that the town clock was wrong and demanded that Serge do something about it. Realising, too late, that the coins were used because they were a precise weight, he begged some from the town treasurer. Desperately, he tried to perform the calculations needed to return the clock to the correct hour, but he became hopelessly lost in a sea of figures, diagrams, and equations. The townsfolk began to lose patience with him, and eventually, they came clamouring to the castle door, demanding to see him. He was afraid. What could he do to appease them? Their cries became louder and angrier. They were threatening to break down the door and pull Serge out when a small, slight, insignificant-looking man who had squeezed his way to the front of the crowd stood and faced them.

"Leave him to me," he said quietly.

Soon, the people quietened down and began to drift away as the news spread. The Time Master was back.

The new part was fitted immediately, and in a few days, the town clock was restored to its former accuracy. People set their timepieces once again with confidence and continued their daily lives with order restored.

As for poor Serge, he was reduced to performing the most menial tasks to teach him the importance of responsibility. Which, if the truth be told, he had already learnt. Persevering, though, he was eventually restored to his former position of trust from which, with time, he progressed to succeed Ardit as Time Master himself. But he never forgot this experience and made sure his apprentice didn't either.

Surreal Events

DORRANCOURT

"Uncle Robbie, I've lost my bracelet," cried a child anxiously across the sand.

Robert Harper, a Council archivist, had brought his niece to West Kirby beach to allow his sister the luxury of shopping in peace. The little girl puckered her face. Rob looked in the hole she'd dug.

"It's ok, Jenny. I'm sure we can get it back." He cleared some loose sand with her spade and straightaway hit something wooden.

The child pointed to a rectangular opening. "It went down that black hole."

The gap was too small to admit a hand, even a child's. Rob lit a match, dropped it through, and saw a glint of silver before the flame spluttered out in the wet sand. The bracelet appeared to have fallen into an old packing case. He looked up. The tide would be in soon.

"I can't get it now, pet. I need a big shovel, like Daddy's, but I'll come back tomorrow, I promise."

He marked the spot by digging in a large clump of seaweed, hoping it wouldn't get washed away, and took several photographs of the location. The silver bracelet had been given to his niece at a wedding, and she couldn't be parted from it. Tears were imminent.

"Why don't we go and get an ice cream?" Come on, let's count my footsteps to the cabin."

Sure enough, the following morning, Rob returned to look for the bracelet, but the retreating sea had left an unusually copious amount of seaweed behind; his search seemed hopeless. He could remember roughly where it was lost, but how could he find that particular spot, even supposing that clump of seaweed was still there? Suddenly, he stumbled into a hole. He uttered an expletive. Could it be Jenny's? It was worth a look. At last, Rob's spade struck the old packing case, but, somewhat intrigued by it, instead of simply breaking through, he decided to dig it out complete, and the more he exposed, the less like a packing case it looked. His excavations finally revealed a large, badly weathered dolls' house, and inside, to the subsequent delight of his niece, Rob found the silver bracelet.

In his spare room, which he was decorating, the dolls' house took pride of place on the wallpaper-pasting table. Deciding to restore the little house, Rob carefully cleaned away the years of sediment and decay with a spatula and brush. Though badly weathered, some shadowy letters became visible over the front door. *D – RR – NC O – RT.* Rob remembered, looking around with his parents, a big old house that was coming under the hammer prior to demolition. He was about fourteen at the time. They were hoping to find bargains for their new home, having just moved from Dumfries to the Wirral. He had forgotten its name but was surprised at how much of the place he could recall, particularly a large painting of an old-time sea captain. By some extraordinary coincidence, this model appeared to be a close replica. The scullery, for instance, he was sure he could find that again, and there it was, complete with all its pots, pans, and utensils. Clearing out the little rooms was as compelling as exploring a real house. All kinds of miniature objects came to light from the grime; a candlestick, a little copper warming pan, crockery, and, though the soft furnishings had perished long ago, some wooden furniture still survived. In the attic, he found a bundle of what remained of oiled silk round waxed paper. Carefully unwrapping it, he found inside, swaddled together like so many tiny mummies, the dolls; three adults and two children. Four of them were obviously a family, while the other adult of African appearance may have been a servant. Drawn again to the letters above the door, the name suddenly came to him; *Dorrancourt*.

Caught unawares at the return of these childhood memories of a house long gone, Rob felt a thrill which compelled him to spend every minute he could restoring it. After a week of painstaking work, much of the cleaning was finished. Repair and redecoration were next. Engrossed in this task, Rob noticed a faint, intermittent noise, almost like whispering. It was still there the next day, louder, even more like whispering. There had to be a rational explanation, but Rob's enquiries of the neighbours proved unproductive while, over the next few days, the frequency and volume of the whispering increased, emanating undeniably, from the dolls' house. Rob shook his head. He couldn't think straight. He'd been too intent on this pursuit. Feeling he must have a complete time out, he took a weekend break in a cottage in North Wales, which was no more than an hour's drive away, hoping the air would clear his mind.

Rob returned with a fresh outlook. How foolish he had been to allow his obsession with the dolls' house to become so intense. He would socialise more with his friends and only allow himself a set amount of time each day for the project, but, to begin with, he wouldn't even permit himself entry into the spare room until he felt in complete control. Nevertheless, the little house began to dominate his thoughts once more. The whispering: there was definitely something uncanny about it. One evening, tempted to turn the handle, he tentatively opened the door. He was about to cross the threshold when fear gripped him. Incredibly, lights were on in the dolls' house; and did he really see the shadow of someone moving in one of its rooms? He shut the door abruptly with a bang, gasping. He would demolish it and dump the infernal thing back in the sea. He grabbed a hammer but hesitated, all the time and care he'd spent on it. No, no arguments; he must smash it now and get rid of it. Opening the spare room door, he was suddenly aware of the time pips broadcast from the radio in his kitchen:

"Good evening. Here is the news at eight o'clock, Saturday, the 25th of June."

*   *   *

"Good evening. Here is the news at eight o'clock, Saturday, the 25th of June."

The voice faded away as Rob heard the door close behind him. He ran to it, but it was jammed. Was this his flat? He rubbed his eyes, opened them again, and looked around. He was in a substantial rectangular hall. Several passageways and doors led from it, and an elegant staircase swept down from a spacious landing. A weird feeling of déjà vu overwhelmed him. Was he losing his mind? In a panic, he gave one of the windows a violent blow with his hammer, to no effect. The bang, however, brought down a sophisticated-looking woman in her mid-forties wearing a slim-line, calf-length dress of embroidered silk crepe. She reminded Rob of an old photograph he'd once seen.

"Excuse me," she said. "What do you think you're doing?"

"Trying to get out,"

"You won't, I'm afraid. All the doors and windows are completely impenetrable."

"What's going on here? Where the hell am I?"

She looked at him with distaste. "This is *Dorrancourt*, and I am Ruth Dorran."

Dorrancourt, of course, he recognised it now.

"I should like to know what you are doing in my house."

Rob was silent for a moment,

"Well, I'm waiting."

He decided to go along with this surreal situation.

"Er, I'm the repairman."

With a rather perplexed look, the woman glanced at something further along the landing that he couldn't see. She looked back again at him.

"Who are you?"

"My name is Robert Harper. As I said, I'm the repairman."

"I see. We've been expecting you. Wait here," and she hastened through one of the doors.

Alone, Rob surveyed his surroundings; a large porcelain vase in one corner, a bust in another, a grandfather clock, a Persian carpet, and several paintings. He crept up the stairs to see what had intrigued Mrs Dorran, and his gaze met the portrait he had seen as a boy. Circa nineteenth-century, he guessed; rather swashbuckling, but that stare! The resemblance to Rob was quite striking. As he returned down the stairs, a gentleman entered, wearing a brown cashmere lounge suit with wide, straight-hanging trousers.

"Come down. Who do you think you are, snooping about private property?"

"Sorry, I meant no harm. I was just curious. My name's Robert Harper. I'm the repairman."

"I know. I'm Craig Dorran. The Master of Dorrancourt. You'll go only where I tell you in future."

"Yes, sir."

"Very well, follow me. Some panels need attention in the Oak Room."

Rob was shown into a rather austere room of dark oak.

"You can begin here. As you see, these ones are badly damaged. See me when you have finished."

"I didn't expect to start right away. I just came to assess the situation, but now I find I can't get out."

"Oh no, there's no escape. In fact, I don't know how you got in here. You're the first new person we've seen since...."

His voice tailed off.

"Never mind. Your clothes are rather odd."

Rob was wearing a t-shirt, jeans, and trainers.

"Are you American? You don't sound like one. Anyway, what sort of a workman are you, coming without your tools?"

"I've got a hammer," said Rob.

"Not much use on its own, is it? I suggest you look in the scullery. This way."

He showed Rob to a kitchen with discoloured walls and a quarry tiled floor. Leading from it was a scullery housing a large sink and laundry equipment. An attractive woman of African or perhaps West Indian descent was rubbing some clothes on a washboard.

"This is Melanie," said Mr Dorran. "Help this fellow, can you?"

Then he turned and left, obviously expecting Rob to get on with his job.

"He says you may have some tools here?" Rob began.

"There's a box in one of those cupboards," Melanie said as she carried on with her work. The light from a nearby window defined, in the forgiving texture of her face, the contours etched by daily toil.

"What's all this about?" Rob asked, rummaging through a small chest containing basic carpentry paraphernalia.

The woman looked puzzled.

"You know, the old fashioned clothes and such."

"Don't let the master and the missus hear you say that. They are the latest nineteen twenty-six fashions."

"Nineteen twenty-six? Have I stepped into some kind of time warp?"

"Time warp?"

"I thought it was science fiction, but. . ."

"You mean like H. G. Wells writes?"

"Sort of."

Rob could just about cope with this idea, but why the impassable doors and windows?

"We've been like this since the wreck," said Melanie.

"Wreck? You mean a shipwreck?"

"Yes. The master's business failed. He had to sell *Dorrancourt* and booked a passage from Liverpool to New Zealand in the hope of starting a new life, but they never arrived. A terrific storm wrecked the ship on sandbanks in Liverpool Bay."

"They were lucky to survive."

"They didn't. The whole family drowned."

Rob's mind seemed to clutch at straws.

"Does that mean they're ghosts?"

"You could say that."

"How did you get here then?"

"I was their servant and went down with them."

"So you're a ghost too?"

"I suppose so."

"You're the prettiest ghost I've ever seen."

Melanie smiled.

"The other servants were dismissed."

"The place is beautifully furnished," said Rob. "You wouldn't know it had fallen on hard times."

"Oh no; all the good stuff was sold."

"But it looks. . ." Rob began, quite bewildered,

"We're living in the dolls' house; the family took it with them. Sentimental reasons, I suppose. It's a copy of the real one. Somehow our souls got trapped in it."

"So you have to do all the work?" said Rob.

"Well, things here aren't quite as they seem," explained Melanie. "Each morning is a kind of return to the previous day."

Rob shook his head in dismay, wondering if he was dead also, and told her how he'd got in. Melanie sighed, saying he was the first new face she'd seen in a very long time and looked strangely pensive.

"Mm, maybe you're the one," she murmured.

Rob returned to the Oak Room. A mahogany table stood in the centre with a matching set of dining chairs and a carver at the head. On the walls were paintings featuring long-ago naval battles and dour portraits of formidable ancestors. He doubted if he would have much appetite with them leering down. A large sideboard occupied one end of the room. He opened it carefully. Inside were silver serving dishes and cut glass decanters. Hearing footsteps, he closed the door quickly and made out he was working. Two children came in and scrutinised him. Realising he must look rather strange, he smiled at them and tried to put them at their ease.

"Hello, who are you?"

"I'm James Dorran," replied the boy, then pointed to his companion. "This is my sister Dora."

He looked about ten years old and the girl no more than seven.

"Are you the repairman?"

"That's right. My name's Rob. Pleased to meet you both."

Just then, the door of the sideboard swung silently open.

"That only happens if someone opens it and forgets to put the paper back when they close it," said James.

"I was looking for some polish," said Rob.

The little boy spoke quietly, in a rather threatening manner.

"You won't find any there. I know what you were doing. Come on, Dora," and they left, their footsteps fading down the passageway.

Desperate, he looked at the windows. Hell, there must be a way out. He gave one of them a hefty crack with a mallet, but it wasn't even marked, and the dark walls loomed up around him like a mausoleum.

Rob repaired the panels with the few tools and scant material he had. After a couple of hours, he considered he deserved a break and made his way to the kitchen. On reaching the hall, he took a detour up to the landing for another look at the portrait. Studying it, he was suddenly aware of Ruth watching him.

"That's Isaac Dorran, my husband's ancestor. He built *Dorrancourt*."

Rob gave a start.

"He's a good looking lad," he said. "In the Navy, was he?"

"He was a naval captain before making his fortune trading overseas."

"What did he trade in?"

"Oh, livestock," she said quickly. "He lost his life when his ship sank off the Ivory Coast."

Meals seemed real enough, and during lunch, Rob asked Melanie where she was from.

"My parents came from Jamaica, looking for work. I was eight at the time. My father got a job in a factory at the docks but was killed in an accident there some years later."

"That must have been very hard for you and your mother."

"I went into service with the Dorrans; she worked in a cotton mill and died of consumption a few months before we set sail." Melanie brushed away a tear.

"You've had a rough time," Rob said, but she dismissed the suggestion.

"No more than other folk."

That night Melanie showed Rob a cramped basic room in the attic where he was to sleep. Light from a candle flickered on her appealing face.

"May I kiss you?"

She didn't resist, and he gently drew her lips to his. They were soft, and she seemed too fragile for servile work

"Thank you for coming. It's been so lonely here," she whispered. "Goodnight," then slipped into the adjoining room.

Rob could hardly believe it. Was he really falling for a ghost?

Sunshine, leaking from a skylight, touched his face. Where was he? Rob had hoped to wake up back at home and, despairingly, wondered if he would ever get away from this claustrophobic place. Waiting for him in the hall, Mr Dorran pulled a fob watch from his waistcoat pocket.

"What time do you call this? I expected you hours ago. You'd better get some breakfast, then see me in the morning room, and don't be long."

Irritated, Rob didn't see why he should take this. But how do you argue with a ghost? He mumbled an apology.

"Don't make a habit of it," said Mr Dorran walking smartly down one of the passageways.

Rob began to calm down as Melanie served him a bowl of porridge. She was the only friendly face around.

"What do you know about Isaac Dorran?" he asked.

"Very little," she said, "except that he was in the Navy and that he had this house built. You look very much like him."

The morning room looked out on a dismal garden with a high hedge beyond which nothing else could be seen. There came a knock at the door. Mr Dorran put his newspaper down as Melanie showed Rob in.

"Mr Harper, sir."

Mr Dorran scowled.

"You took your time. Have you finished in the Oak Room?"

"As far as I can under the circumstances."

"Very well, the floor needs attention in one of the bedrooms. Follow me."

He led the way back into the hall and up the stairs.

"He's a fine chap, your ancestor," remarked Rob as they passed the portrait. "What kind of livestock did he trade in?"

"It's none of your business," said Mr Dorran curtly.

"I'm just interested," Rob persisted. "Seeing that he looks so much like me."

"Yes, I believe he had an illegitimate child. The birth was never registered. Descent from it wouldn't be anything to be proud of."

Why was this man so belligerent, so infuriating? Rob bit his tongue.

"My wife uses this as a dressing room," said Mr Dorran.

He pointed out some rotten floorboards and then left. On the bed, crisp, white, starched sheets were turned down from plump pillows. Close by, there was a marble-topped washstand holding a porcelain basin and jug. Near the window stood a dressing table in walnut veneer and a matching wardrobe opposite housing some very expensive-looking furs, mink, seal, and ocelot, along with sequined ball gowns. He turned to begin his work and noticed Dora standing in the doorway.

"Those are mummy's evening gowns. What are you doing?"

"Checking for moths," said Rob.

"James was right about you," she said, then left.

He ran to the door, "I can explain...," but she had gone.

On his way to the kitchen, Rob heard raised voices coming from the lounge.

"What were you thinking of Ruth? We know nothing about him, who he is or where he comes from. He's the last person you should say anything to; worse still, you told him Isaac was a livestock trader on the Ivory Coast. He's bound to put two and two together. Whatever possessed you?"

"There's no reason why he should suspect Isaac had anything to do with slaves, still less the Dorran curse."

"Just keep a guard on your tongue in future. I don't want him privy to our family skeletons."

"Don't shout so, Craig. You're giving me a headache. I'm going up to my room."

Hiding in the shadow of the grandfather clock, Rob watched Mrs Dorran hurry up the stairs to her chamber. So that was Isaac Dorran's business. Slaves. The thought was chilling enough, but what was the curse? Melanie admitted to Rob that she knew about Isaac Dorran's business, but Mr Dorran had made her keep quiet about it.

"Please don't say anything," she pleaded; "he'll be terribly angry."

Regarding the curse, however, she could not be drawn, and Rob did not want to stress her further.

On his return to the bedroom, Rob was soon conscious of James watching him; the boy gave him the creeps.

"Are you still doing repairs?"

"Yes," said Rob.

"You look like that man in the painting."

"Do I? Can you tell me anything about it?"

"No,"

"I believe it has something to do with a curse?"

67

The boy gave him a quizzical look and left. Presently, Mrs Dorran came in.

"I can't find my pearls. I don't suppose you've seen them, have you?"

"No, I haven't," said Rob.

Ruth searched the dressing table drawers but without success.

"I'll have another look on my bedside table," and so saying, she left to continue her quest.

About half an hour later, James returned.

"Father wants to see you in his study. I'll show you where it is."

They came to a rather gloomy corner on the ground floor.

"Father always keeps it locked if he isn't in," said James as he knocked on a foreboding-looking door.

"Come in," came a cold voice.

"The repairman is here, Father."

"Very well, show him in."

Rob walked into a small cheerless room; with heavy drapes at the window and shelves of fading old books, among which he noticed a time-worn collection of journals under the heading, *Family History*.

"What's the problem?" Rob asked as cheerily as he could.

Mr Dorran looked up from his desk.

"I think you know where my wife's pearls are."

"What makes you think that?"

"I believe you've been snooping in the cupboards and drawers."

"If you think I've taken them, I assure you I haven't. Anyway, why would I want them shut in this place?"

Mr Dorran pursed his lips; "I imagine only you would know that."

He took a service revolver from his desk.

"But if I find you've been pilfering, I'll have no compunction in shooting you like a dog. Now get out!"

Rob left the study with a sinking feeling in the pit of his stomach. Nevertheless, he suspected the answers to his questions lay in those journals, but if James was right, accessing them would not be easy. Rob decided that the only way to get to them was to persuade Mr Dorran to leave his study because of some crisis or other, hoping that he would neglect to lock it.

In the bedroom where he had been working, Rob found an empty bottle smelling faintly of roses and a fox fur collar sporting its head and legs. He smiled to himself as the germ of an idea formed in his mind. The very thing. It might just work. The door of the bedroom opposite was open just enough for him to see Mrs Dorran brushing her hair. Quietly, he pinned the fox fur from the lintel by the base of its tail so that it hung down at eye level. He concealed himself in the hall behind a large chair in sight of the study and rolled the bottle across the wooden floor. Disturbed by the noise, Mr Dorran came out to upbraid the culprit.

"James? Dora?"

Then he found the bottle and called his wife.

"Ruth, Ruth. What's going on?"

Soon there came a shriek as Mrs Dorran encountered the fox fur collar. At this, Craig Dorran marched swiftly up the stairs, allowing Rob time to slip into the study. The journals filled a couple of shelves; manuscripts, hardbound in worn, claret-coloured linen. He chose the volumes dating from 1800 to 1900 and spread the others out to make the gap less obvious. Footsteps signalled Craig's return, grim-faced and accompanied by his wife, as Rob scurried furtively into the Oak Room to avoid them, but Mr Dorran looked in.

"I thought you'd finished here?"

"Sorry," Rob replied, crouching on the floor to conceal the journals, "There's a bit I've missed,"

"Tradesmen, Ruth. Sloppy; not like they used to be."

Rob hid the journals in the scullery, studying them at night to avoid suspicion. The first volume appeared fruitless until one entry, written in an untidy copperplate, caught his eye:

Monday, March 30th, 1807: Damnation! Parliament has voted to abolish slavery from May 1st and is planning to send out naval vessels to patrol the West coast of Africa. There's got to be a way of getting around this, or I shall be finished.
Isaac Dorran.

"His very own writing," murmured Rob to himself.

Further on, he recognized another entry in the same hand.

Sunday, September 20th. 1812 The situation is worsening. About three months ago, I loaded my ship at Lagos. Despite sailing under Portuguese colours, we were pursued by the British naval patrol ship H.M.S Amelia. She has a formidable reputation, so I ordered the cargo to be thrown overboard. The slaves weren't worth the stiff fine I would have incurred had I been caught with them. One sullen brute pointed his finger directly at me and gabbled some incomprehensible nonsense. My first mate, knowing something of their language, told me I'd been cursed. This might work on primitive savages, but not modern civilized people. All is perfectly well here as I sit and write this journal at Dorrancourt.
Isaac Dorran.

Sickened by this sheer disregard for humanity, Rob continued and discovered an entry by Isaac's brother.

Wednesday, August 4th. 1813: My brother Isaac, R.I.P., lost his life when his ship foundered off the Ivory Coast last June. Having inherited Dorrancourt, I have set up home here with my wife Bertha and our two sons, Daniel and Jeremy.
Jacob Dorran.

Rob gave a quick intake of breath. Strange! Isaac drowned almost one year to the day he was cursed. Peppered throughout the succeeding volumes were entries giving accounts concerning the first-born sons in

71

the family; all had drowned in one way or another. Some were in their sixties, but many were much younger, one of the first being Daniel Dorran who died in a boating accident while a student at Cambridge University; another, still in his infancy, drowned in a garden pond, and his mother wrote bitterly:

Oh, Isaac, we are paying dearly for your guilt.

Rob knit his brows; God, how awful to have a thing like that hanging over your family!

In a later volume, he noticed it, a reference to the picture.

<u>Saturday, November 14th, 1874:</u> Last night, I contacted my great Grandfather Isaac through a medium. We now know the truth of the curse. Lydia is very upset and will not have his picture in the hall a moment longer. We have agreed to move it to the landing. Madam Alkaev foretold the curse would only be broken by a stranger with a strong resemblance to Isaac. I pray to God he will come soon. The funeral of our eldest son Henry took place last week.
Philip Dorran.

So that was why Melanie said he might be the one, but what was he expected to do?

The next day, hearing screams from the kitchen, Rob found Mr Dorran beating Melanie with a Malacca cane.

"I told you not to say anything. How dare you disobey me?"

Filled with revulsion, Rob grabbed him by the shoulder and pulled him away.

"Come on, tough guy. Try me instead."

"Mind your own business," snapped Craig, swiping at him with the cane.

Rob, however, caught it and pulled it from his grasp.

"Now," he said. "See how you like it."

"You will regret this, mark my words," said Mr Dorran, as he tried to regain his dignity.

"Get out of here," said Rob, driving him from the kitchen.

Melanie was shaking, her sobs coming in great spasms.

"Are you badly hurt?" he asked.

"Not much. I'll be ok," but he could see the wheals swelling on her legs.

"Those are nasty. Let me wash them for you."

She succumbed, and he bathed them as gently as he could.

Smarting and humiliated, Mr Dorran returned to his study, brooding on what action to take. He returned a book to its place and noticed some of the journals were missing.

"Very well," he muttered to himself as he opened a drawer in his desk. "I'll deal with this repairman."

"See, this is the first reference to the picture I've found," said Rob, showing Melanie one of the volumes. "Jacob Dorran mentions discovering it in the cellar in 1815, and he had it displayed in the hall in memory of his brother."

Footsteps were heard in the passageway.

"Quick," said Melanie. "Hide it."

She opened a cupboard as Craig Dorran entered.

"I warned you," he said. "I will not tolerate pilferers in my house."

Without further restraint, he drew his pistol; Melanie screamed, and a single shot rent the air.

*   *   *

"You're safe now," said a voice.

Rob slowly came round, looking into the face of a Salvation Army officer.

"Melanie, Melanie."

"He's calling for you," said the officer to a black woman in a similar uniform.

"But I don't know him," she said. "I've never met him before."

"Oh, Melanie, thank God you're safe."

Rob looked around. His chest hurt, but there was no trace of a wound.

"Where are we?"

"You're in a Salvation Army refuge. We found you slumped in an alleyway, but how do you know my name?"

"How did we get out?" said Rob. "We were living in *Dorrancourt*. Mr Dorran beat you, then shot me."

"I've no idea who you are," said Melanie, but Mr Dorran wouldn't do such a thing; besides, the family

74

don't live in *Dorrancourt* anymore. They're in a hotel in Liverpool, waiting to board a ship to New Zealand."

"You're not a ghost?"

"Lord bless you, no,"

"Then it's not too late. You mustn't go with them."

"But I'm their maid. Mr Dorran was good enough to keep me on when the house was sold. I can't give up my job, not as how things are these days."

"You mustn't go," Rob insisted. "Neither must they." Melanie looked blankly at him, so Rob related everything he knew about her.

"It's not possible," she said incredulously. "How can you know all this? The only thing I can suggest is that you speak to Mr Dorran himself. I could take you to see him this afternoon, but I must say none of this makes any sense to me."

The afternoon sun lent a glow to the smog that pervaded the city streets. They were just as Rob had seen them in pictures of old Liverpool. He recognised many of the landmarks, some of which he had only seen in photographs, and he tried to place where others would be built in years to come. They eventually arrived at a modest hotel near Lime Street Station, and on meeting the Dorrans, Rob found none of the malevolence he had encountered previously; rather, they were a normal friendly family.

"This is not a social visit," said Rob urgently. "You mustn't board that ship."

Try as he might, there seemed no way of convincing them of the impending tragedy. Even though he described *Dorrancourt* in as much detail as he could, Mr Dorran was adamant they were going,

"I really can't call a halt to the proceedings on such feeble evidence. I have invested a good deal of my capital in this venture. We expect to board any day now. Our possessions will be loaded on *The Southern Cross* first thing tomorrow morning."

Rob couldn't understand how this man could put his son in such danger, but then perhaps he'd had lost an older son. When he mentioned the curse, Craig was suddenly attentive.

"How do you know about it? Nobody knows about the curse except my wife and I."

"Look, I know it's hard to believe," Rob persisted, "but I really am from the future." The future; yes, of course, his smartphone; that might just prove it. He felt in his pocket. Would it still be there? How much of it would work? "You see this?"

Mr Dorran examined the phone sceptically.

"It's from the twenty-first century and only recognises my fingerprint."

At his touch, it sprang into life, and he managed to demonstrate some of its applications, the video camera and the music player.

"It's a telephone as well," said Rob. "The infrastructure isn't in place yet, but it works fine where I come from."

While they watched, amazed, Craig said thoughtfully, "The twenty-first century, you say? On a visit to the Central Library a few days ago, I came across an article in *Colliers Weekly*, an American magazine. It contained an interview with an eminent electrical engineer, name of Nikola Tesla, in which he predicted the development of just such a device."

"My husband is in the same line of business," said Ruth.

"Father," James quietly interjected. "He looks like the man in the picture."

"By George, you're right, the stranger," said Mr Dorran.

Gradually his conviction grew. Craig put an immediate halt to loading his luggage, though, unfortunately, the dolls' house had already been taken on board and could not be retrieved. For days, Rob, and Craig, did their utmost to warn the authorities of the impending disaster. The captain was immovable.

"I can't possibly be influenced in this manner. This is a state-of-the-art vessel. The chances of her sinking are minimal, and if you try to upset my passengers, I'll have you arrested. Now leave; I've got a ship to command."

Trying to change history was impossible. Even so, a shadow seemed to have lifted from Craig Dorran's face. The curse would be broken at last. His children would be free.

Ruth sighed. "We have a lot to thank you for. Is there any way we can repay you?"

"I'd like to study the picture further," replied Rob.

"The developers who bought *Dorrancourt* agreed to keep it there as part of the property," Craig added. "There may be someone to let you in. Here, take this.

It's not much, but it should, at least, cover transport and some lodging. You have done us a great service. The family will be forever grateful."

On arrival at *Dorrancourt*, Rob lifted the large knocker. The door opened slightly. He pushed it further and, hesitantly, crept in.

*   *   *

Time pips sounded. "Good evening. Here is the news at eight o'clock. Saturday, June the twenty-fifth."

The radio! He was back home. There was the dolls' house and the wrappings, but the dolls were gone.

*   *   *

"I'm Robert Harper. I've come to visit Mrs Sutcliffe."

"Enter," said the intercom.

The nursing home door buzzed and let Rob in.

"Ah, yes," said the sister. She's been expecting you. Quite excited, though I don't understand what she's talking about."

Rob was shown into a comfortable sitting room with a pleasant aspect.

"I've been so looking forward to meeting you again," said an elderly lady sitting in an easy chair. "It's amazing; you don't look a day older than when I saw you all those years ago. Have you still got that wonderful instrument?"

Rob brought out his smartphone.

"Right here, Dora."

"We owe you a great deal. Unfortunately, *the Southern Cross* was wrecked, just as you said, with terrible loss of life."

She held a yellowing scrap of newspaper in her arthritic fingers. The headline ran *Liner Tragedy in Liverpool bay*. Chatting over tea and cake, Rob enquired about her brother.

"James joined the Navy; he fought in the Second World War, which, thankfully, he survived. He died peacefully in his sleep about fifteen years ago."

To Dora's amazement, Rob wheeled in a trolley bearing the dolls' house he had restored.

"It's just the same," she said wistfully. "It was kept in the nursery, but I was only allowed to play with it on Sundays. What will you do with it?"

"Well, it's really yours," said Rob."

"Then I suggest it be auctioned to raise funds for aid in Africa,"

Rob agreed wholeheartedly and promised to make the necessary arrangements.

"Out of interest," he said as he took his leave, "have you any idea what happened to Melanie?"

"All I know is, she met a Jamaican sailor. Name of Brooks and returned with him to the West Indies."

Sitting once more on West Kirby beach, Rob reflected on all he'd been through. He missed Melanie, her warm smile, and gentle voice. He had to admit, though, that even if he combed the entire Caribbean and married one of her descendants, he would always be in love with a ghost. His reverie was broken, however, by a familiar cry from across the sand.

"Uncle Robbie!"

THE IRISH GIANT

My name is Lucas, and I am a freelance journalist. I originally wrote much of this account many years ago as a statement for the police while I was detained in a cell in Northern Ireland. They didn't accept it, however, because part of it seems quite implausible, but I feel it is high time I wrote a complete account for the people of Tobercraigy. Included are other inexplicable events, the credibility of which I leave to the reader.

I had begun a new job as a technician in the Department of Human Pathology at a university in the north of England. I was looking forward to the different experiences and attractive salary this advancement in my career would bring.

On my first day, my immediate superior, Dr Elizabeth Nixon, took me on a department tour and introduced me to the people I would be working with. After this preliminary induction, she showed me to my office, an annexe to a sizable laboratory where students and researchers conducted the practical aspects of their studies. Here, I would be readily available to cater to their needs.

"These are the keys to your kingdom," said Dr Nixon as she presented me with a bunch that opened the doors of the lab, my office, and, for the times when I would be required to work weekends, the front door. A distinct chemical smell identified the room, and our footsteps echoed on the grey-painted floor, scuffed here and there by the movement of stools and equipment. The sinks in the long benches were multi-coloured from years of preparing microscope slides, and their teak tops carried stains that told a similar story. One key on the bunch opened some glass-fronted display cabinets around the walls, containing a comprehensive collection of human organs and other body parts preserved mainly in jars of formalin. Another gave access to drawers below that held an immense library of stained specimens of diseased tissue on microscope slides.

In a corner opposite the office stood a very tall, narrow cabinet. Intrigued by this, I asked Dr Nixon what it could possibly contain. Without a word, she unlocked the door. As it swung open, I gasped at the sight of what must have been one of the largest human skeletons in existence, fully eight feet tall, perhaps nearer nine.

"That," she said, "is our Irish giant."

I had the impression that it looked down at me with a pitiable stare; if you could call it a stare, almost as if it were begging for something. I stood there for what seemed like an age, completely dumbfounded, but it could only have been a few seconds until Dr Nixon spoke again in quite a straightforward manner.

"It is an excellent example of gigantism, which, as you probably know, is caused by the overproduction of growth hormone during childhood."

"What do you know about him?" I asked at length. "His history?"

"All I can tell you," she replied, "is that he lived in Northern Ireland. He came from the medical school of a university in the south of England, where he originally belonged to a Professor Wagstaff, who worked there in the late nineteenth century. It's extremely valuable. Even if it were possible to buy such a specimen nowadays, it would be quite unaffordable."

"How did you acquire him?" I asked.

"I believe he was brought here as an exhibit for an endocrinology symposium in the 1950s and has stayed ever since on permanent loan. We are very fortunate to have him. He is often used in teaching and even research."

Part of my responsibility was to curate this collection of examples and curiosities. So I decided I would begin by making an inventory of them all with a view to producing a catalogue and database in the order that each item and related samples could be readily located.

My fascination with the skeleton did not diminish, and after several months I took a break during which I drove down to visit the medical school where it had originally come from to see what I could glean from their archives.

I trawled through reams of irrelevant documents looking for some notes or references to the skeleton and finally came across a dusty tome written by Professor Wagstaff. In it was an account of the techniques he had used in preparing the skeleton, which he carried out while working in Liverpool. This was accompanied by detailed anatomical drawings of the various body parts and systems as they had been revealed during the process, as well as drawings of the skeleton itself which he named Sean Rafferty. I was in no doubt that these were portrayals of the actual skeleton in my care because somehow, the artist had captured the same pitiable begging expression by which I had been transfixed.

I discovered that Sean had died at the Liverpool Royal Infirmary, which at the time was on Brownlow Hill. As the Giant appeared to have no immediate relatives, Wagstaff, whose patient he had been, claimed the body for medical science as an exceptional example of hormone imbalance and later took the skeleton with him to the Medical School where he had secured a professorship in endocrinology.

On my return home, I obtained a reference number from the Free BMD (Births Marriages, and Deaths) Database and arranged online for a copy of the death certificate to be posted to me. This arrived a week later and stated that Sean Rafferty had died at the age of twenty-eight on the nineteenth of September 1875, in the Liverpool Royal Infirmary, having been a labourer at the Princes Dock. The cause of death was given as heart failure and signed by Dr Wagstaff, as he was then.

The thought occurred to me that because of his size, Rafferty must have been something of a celebrity, at least among his work-mates at the Princes Dock, and it would not be beyond the bounds of possibility for there to be a newspaper article about him. I searched the internet for a promising local paper and eventually came across the Liverpool Mercury.

I paid a month's subscription to the British Newspaper Archive and put in a search online with the scant data I had. I found information relating to the hard life of dock labourers, as well as matters relating to shipping and business. Obituaries were also in abundance, but who, in those days, wrote such eulogies about dockers? Nothing turned up that was of any significant help, and I was beginning to wonder if, in fact, anyone had ever taken any notice of him. I eventually decided, as a last-ditch attempt, to naively include the keyword - giant. At that, the name almost jumped out at me. The article was more than I could have hoped for. An interview with Sean Rafferty himself. It had been written by a reporter named Mary Doolan who, determined not to allow the passing of this extraordinary man to go unnoticed, had visited him in hospital during his final illness to record first-hand his memories of the life he had led.

She portrayed his childhood in Tobercraigy, a small town in County Antrim, where he was raised as the adopted son of a publican. In her account, she describes him as a familiar and normal part of community life but also as a solitary soul seeking respite in the countryside around his home. At the age of eleven, he left school to work for his father at the pub. Later he hired himself out to neighbouring farmers and builders for some of the heavier jobs. Sean's adoptive parents had a daughter a few years younger than him, and there came a time when he began to be troubled by amorous feelings for her. A small circus was touring the district at that time –

Riley's Big Top Spectacular. As the situation at home became more difficult, to avoid scandal and further anguish, Sean joined it and became a popular part of the programme. One thing he refused to do, though, was to wear glitzy show clothes, preferring those that looked more familiar and ordinary so that people would understand he was as human as they were and not a mere freak.

After a couple of years, he sailed for Liverpool with the circus and toured the surrounding district. Eventually, however, life performing as a public curiosity began to pall and even annoy him. Some people asked insensitive questions, and others even kicked his legs to see if they were real. He retreated from their jibes and gawps whenever he could, and on the return of Riley's Big Top Spectacular to Ireland, he stayed on in Liverpool as a dock labourer. During the interview, he spoke with nostalgia about his life in County Antrim, how he loved the wild places around the Giant's Causeway, the salty, tangy smell of the sea, the bracing air and spindrift in his face. Realising he was nearing the end of his life, his final wish was to be returned home.

My routine in the lab continued as usual. One evening I was working late, setting out equipment and various specimens, ready for an examination the following morning. As I went about these preparations, I mulled over the information I had collected concerning the Giant and decided to take another look at him. I opened the cabinet and gazed up at him for several minutes, thinking of the life he must have led, while, still, he seemed to look down at me with that imploring stare.

"What is it you want of me?" I said quietly.

The last thing I could clearly remember of that evening was preparing to go home. The rest, even now, is still very vague.

As I opened my eyes, I heard a voice say, "Welcome back, Lucas. You had us all quite worried."

Then I recognised Dr Nixon sitting beside me as I lay in a hospital bed.

"What am I doing here?" I asked. "What happened?"

"We were hoping you would be able to give us some idea," she said. "You were found by a security guard, lying on the floor of the Path. Lab. with the Irish Giant in a heap beside you. Whatever were you doing?"

I delved into the recesses of my mind, and a memory began to emerge. Very sketchy at first.

Darkness had fallen outside, and I was looking through some papers when I felt a heavy, uncomfortable grip on my right shoulder. I looked up and, in the reflections of the lab window, distinctly caught sight of a large skeleton towering behind me. I looked over to the giant's cabinet. It was open and empty. Was it my imagination? I froze as, from the very corner of my eye, I could just make out the tips of some large bony digits. A voice, whether physical or in my mind, I will never be sure, filtered through the silence in a low whisper, "Take me home."

After that, my memory was a complete blank, and to this day, I cannot recall how I got to the hospital.

As my recollection of this event began to solidify, at least in part, I tentatively re-counted my concept of the incident to Dr Nixon.

"It's quite ridiculous," she said. "How can you possibly take any notice of even a fraction of that, let alone expect anyone else to?"

"I'm not sure what to believe," I answered. "I am only relating what is coming to mind. I have no other explanation. All I am certain of is that he must be returned home."

"That's crazy. Even if others should agree with you, the Irish Giant is still a very important feature in our department, and don't forget it doesn't even belong to us. I can't see the university down south subscribing to any such nonsense."

On my return to duty, I went to see the Head of Department, Professor Horner, in his study to try and persuade him to let the skeleton go and showed him the background material I had gathered, but he had no wish even to consider it.

"You're getting obsessed with all this, Lucas," he said. "And we've all noticed your work suffer. Take some time off. We can find cover for you, for a while at least. I suggest you see a psychiatrist. Come back when you've cleared this from your mind."

I thanked him for being so understanding, retrieved a few belongings from my desk, and went home to weigh up what I was to do.

Nothing, however, would silence the voice playing continually in my head.

"Take me home."

I came to the conclusion that the only chance I had of staying sane was at the expense of my career. I, therefore, resolved to steal the skeleton and take it back to County Antrim myself.

I returned to work after a couple of weeks, whereupon I made arrangements with a freight company to pick up a large cabinet at the front door of the Path. Lab. one weekend and transport it to Northern Ireland. There would be little disturbance at that time. No one to see and ask awkward questions. On leaving, I posted the keys through the letter box minus the one to the cabinet, together with my letter of resignation and accompanied the skeleton on its flight.

I had been in touch with Father Michael Kendrick in Rafferty's home town of Tobecraigy and explained to him about the skeleton, emailing him copies of the death certificate and the article from the Liverpool Mercury. He was good enough to accommodate me in his home and the skeleton in the church. He told me that, though there seemed no evidence to support the truth of them, tales and even legends of there having been a colossus in the town still circulated amongst its inhabitants.

"Now that we know his name," he said. "Why don't we look in the parish records to see what else we can find out about him?"

Here, we found that Sean Rafferty had been baptised on May 26th, 1847, as the adopted son of Phileas, and Nora Rafferty, Phileas being the publican of the Antrim

Arms in Tobercraigy, and that the baptism was performed by a Father Aloysius O'Brien.

"Ah, he's still spoken of in this town," said Father Kendrick. "There is a memorial to him in the church and a small booklet published about his life. He was a good man. Seeing as this Sean Rafferty actually existed here, and we have a bit more information about him, it is only right that his remains should have a proper burial."

So, Father Kendrick agreed to perform the ceremony and arranged for the interment of the skeleton in the Rafferty family plot.

Quite a buzz swept the little town at the news that one of its long-lost sons had finally come home. The cabinet, which served well as a coffin, lay open in the parish church the day before the service so that those that wished to could pay their respects. That evening before the interment, Father Kendrick and I went in to close it. Looking at the Giant for the last time and whispering a farewell, I fancied its imploring expression, if there ever can be one in a skeleton, had gone. He was at rest, and for the first time in months, the voice in my head stopped, so I also felt at peace. But it didn't last long because two policemen turned up at the door that night with a warrant to arrest me for the theft of the skeleton. I accompanied them to the police station, answered their questions, and was detained in a cell where I wrote much of this account.

My disappointment at not being able to attend the ceremony was allayed somewhat when the next day, one of the policemen came and informed me that on entering the church that morning, the priest found the cabinet, and its contents had gone. So, as there were no grounds to detain me now, I could no longer be held.

Father Kendrick and I made scrupulous enquiries about this disappearance, particularly among the key-holders of the church, but none of those we questioned had been in there after it was locked the night before, and certainly no one had been allowed in after. There was, however, one person who we were unable to interrogate, the undertaker, a well-respected man in the community, who, for some unknown reason, had not turned up at his shop that morning. We heard later that he had been found by a motorist on the A2 Causeway Coastal Route collapsed next to his hearse. The back of the vehicle was open, and extending out several feet was the Giant's cabinet, gaping and empty. We never discovered who helped load it.

The undertaker died soon after reaching hospital. The diagnosis was a heart attack, and with his last breath, he murmured something sounding like, "He's home; he's home."

So, I was unemployed. Nevertheless, my research into the life of this unusual dock labourer and the account I wrote about returning him to his hometown drew me to the field of journalism, resulting in a change of career. I am now married with a family, and we live in Tobercraigy.

I had been there little more than a year when I noticed an article in a local newspaper headed **Barebones of a Tall Story.** Apparently, a shepherd had taken shelter from the weather in a cave near the Giant's Causeway. As his eyes accommodated to the dim light, he was startled by the sight of an unusually large human skeleton lying among the rocks that littered the cave floor. I spent some time looking for this cave, but as its location was very unclear, and there are numerous caves in the district, I failed to find the one described. During subsequent years there have been occasional reported sightings of an oversized skeletal figure perched on a dark basalt column or standing on the edge of a cliff, looking out across the wide expanse of the Atlantic Ocean. Invariably these sightings have occurred as a silhouette in the face of an approaching storm or against a flaming sunset, and the few available photographs are very grainy and indistinct. Experts and sceptics dismiss it as nothing more than an optical illusion, a trick of the light on an unusual rock formation. Or is there just a possibility it could be Sean Rafferty, home, back in the countryside he loved?

LIFE OF A SALESMAN

A man sits outside a busy street café. He's like any other customer except for the scarring on his face.

"This free?" a smart young man asks him, indicating a vacant seat.

"Sure, you're welcome."

He sits, but doesn't relax, bolts his sandwich, sips hot coffee from a paper cup.

"In a hurry, son?"

"I've got an interview."

"Who with?"

"*Assegai* Sportswear. "

"The South African company."

"You know it?" The young man looks surprised.

"Oh, I know it, alright."

"It'll be a wonderful opportunity."

"Tell me more about it. Another coffee?"

"Must go."

"Why? The job will still be there."

"Possibly, but it won't be mine, and right now, I'm going to do my damnedest to get it."

The scarred man slowly stirs his tea.

"That was me once. Rushing around chasing my tail, but life is deeper than that."

"Maybe," retorts the young man. "But this is important to me, and I'm not here to debate it. Gotta go, or I'll be late."

"Good-bye. I'll see you again," the older man answers

"I doubt it."

The lad hails a cab, and races across the street, dodging blaring horns, his half-finished coffee left cooling on the table. The other man slowly manoeuvres his wheelchair and is lost among the shoppers.

*   *   *

Assegai Sportswear displayed its logo, a silver dart with a scarlet tip, at Birmingham's N.E.C. Here, John Waterman promoted their latest trainers using a well-honed script, skilfully adapting it to any situation. A DVD attracted passers-by, explaining the innovations of the new footwear. A stripped-down sample allowed close examination of its winning qualities.

"Not available on general distribution for another six months," John declared to captivated onlookers, "but here today, at a discount price."

Soon credit cards and cheques flew from convinced by-standers to purchase them.

"Don't worry, madam," he shouted to an eager young woman. "I'll see you take a pair home today."

It was worth a risk sometimes to make sales and boost custom. His comment, "I've a soft spot for the ladies," always produced a titter.

Taking a quick break, John was surprised to meet the young woman who owed him for the trainers. An attractive brunette with hazel eyes.

"Hi, trying to avoid the crush? This bar is reserved for exhibitors."

She smiled. "Actually, I run *Cavalcade*. I'm Ashley Haynes. We print T-shirts, and embroider badges, anything really."

"I see. We, I mean *Assegai,* may use you. All the exhibitors in my hotel are having a meal together on the last night. Would you care to join us?"

Ashley wasn't sure, but John's affable personality won.

The delegates talked shop well into the night. There was good food and good wine.

"Oh, look at the time!" said Ashley anxiously. "The guesthouse will be locked, and I haven't got a key."

"No worries," said John. "Stay in my room. I'll sort things out in the morning."

As a rule, John was up and on the road by six a.m., but he made an exception to settle things for Ashley with the guest house. As usual, he caught up with his e-mails and conducted most of his business at motorway service stations.

After his success at Birmingham's sports fair, he was looking to make a killing at the Dublin show. Passionate about his work, he visited customers and aggressively promoted *Assegai*, finishing around nine in the evening unless he entertained clients, as he often did, at nightclubs and restaurants. He grabbed every opportunity and arranged the removal of anyone that got in his way. He worked his trainees hard and wouldn't tolerate mistakes.

"John, our sales have increased remarkably, thanks to you," said his manager. "We've decided to send you to our headquarters in Durban, where we need you to win the case for *Assegai* to have exclusive rights kitting out the South African Olympic squad. Of course, if you can pull this off, we'll want you at the Games."

While regaling the South African runners, John received a text from Ashley reading simply -

<<Hi John. Your son needs his Daddy. Call back. Love you. >>

"You're popular, John," said a hundred metres hopeful.

"Ah, it's nothing. Some woman after my body. I get 'em all the time."

His guests chuckled, but he had received several texts and voicemails from Ashley during the last year saying she loved him and was pregnant. She wanted to talk with him about their relationship, but he dismissed them.

John watched with pride as the team he had outfitted marched into the Olympic arena sporting the *Assegai* insignia. He attended parties for the gold medal winners and organised promotional events. During one such occasion, another voice mail arrived from Ashley.

"John, Kyle will be starting school next year. I so want you to come with me to meet the teachers. Love you"

Again he disdained it.

"No rest for the wicked," he said to a charmed audience. "Another toast for our champion. Give him a big hand, everybody."

On John's return, an assertive young co-worker had usurped him on the board.

96

"After all that I've done for this company," complained John to the Corporate Chief. "If this is all the thanks I get, I might as well go elsewhere. Several topflight sportswear companies are headhunting me, you know."

"Mr Waterman, you're a greatly valued member of staff."

"Seems like it, sir."

"In fact, we would like to offer you the position of Head of Global Operations."

Yes! Now he'd fix that little pea-brain that had seized his authority while he was away.

One sport that *Assegai* did not supply was motor racing. On his promotion, John employed top designers to create suitable apparel that would provide drivers with as much protection as possible but look stylish. He had them thoroughly tested with dummies using sophisticated equipment measuring impact and fire resistance.

"Do it again," he demanded. "Improve the design. It looks like a Noddy suit. I wouldn't wear that in bed. It must look cool."

An outfit was finally produced that ticked all the boxes. After agreeing to adopt it exclusively, Sagitar Motor Racing Limited would debut it at the Formula One, Rolex, British Grand Prix, at Silverstone.

Waiting for the race to begin, John was chatting to some Sagitar executives when one of the crew interrupted anxiously.

"Sir, Max Heaton can't race. He's had some sort of seizure."

This was serious, he was their foremost driver, and no reserve was available. John thought for a minute.

"I'll do it."

They looked sceptical.

"I've done plenty of car rallying. Come on, give me a break."

Reluctantly they took John to be readied. Passing the pits, one of the technicians noticed him. Pea-brain! He'd better not get in the way.

"Are you comfortable, John?" asked one of the service team.

Yes, he was snug as the proverbial bug, fulfilling his schoolboy dream. Would that gun ever fire?

They were off! He left at a furious pace, taking the lead immediately. He'd show them. The car flew down the track like an arrow, but soon John noticed the temperature gauge rising. Smoke poured into the cockpit, and then flames issued from his bonnet. He careered onto the gravel trap, crashed into the tyre barrier, and burst into an inferno.

"Johnny!" screamed a woman from the crowd as emergency services raced to his rescue.

*   *   *

The fire had gone, I was bathed in a wonderful light. Unlike lamplight or sunlight, this luminescence had infinite intelligence and contained within it the whole of creation and human goodness. Shining through every fibre of my being, it knew me totally. I felt vulnerable and afraid. The Light emanated an ineffable love, love for me. I wanted to stay there forever, but I sensed my negativity burning up. Fearing I may be consumed altogether, I left that awesome presence, sobbing uncontrollably in my anguish as I retreated into darkness.

"He's waking. Nurse, nurse." I heard footsteps. "He's crying. Look at the tears."

In agony, I was gradually eased back into oblivion at the prick of a needle.

For months I endured surgery, skin grafts, and a battle to save my sight.

"I'm Ashley," said a woman at my bedside. "Remember the trainers? Our night together. I sent you texts and voicemails. I even tried to reach you at Silverstone."

What could I say?

"Why should you love me?" I replied. "It was only one night."

"Love has no reason, John."

I couldn't see her for the dressings, but in her, I perceived something of the Bliss I had experienced, and my love for her grew.

Light flooded in as the bandages were removed. Some of my sight had been saved.

"Hello, John," said Ashley. "Can you see much?

"You're rather blurred. I've been told that should pass, but I've only a narrow field of vision."

"John, this is our son." She presented a four-year-old boy. "Kyle, say hello."

He duly did.

"Hello, Kyle. I'm not a pretty sight, am I?"

"Don't worry, Daddy," he said. "I still love you."

Alone in the hospital, I plucked up the courage to look in the mirror. I wheeled myself towards the sink and gasped in shock. I thought I knew what to expect but staring back at me was the face of a man I had met at a street café.

Ashley visited frequently, despite my anger and tears.

"Why me?" I repeated incessantly.

To which she gently replied.

"Why you? Why are you alive when you should be dead?"

I had no answer, but slowly there began in me a process of more positive thinking.

On discharge, the world immediately filled my senses, birdsong, flowers, and sunsets. Everything spoke of the Light I'd encountered.

Ashley and I married, and now every day is a special gift. These days I run a second-hand bookshop, but there's no more hard sell. I listen to people instead. They tell me about themselves, their hopes, fears and problems. Yes, I still have dark times, but I'll be forever thankful that I'm blessed with a new life and a family I do not deserve.

TOWARD A NEW HORIZON

The hour was late as I sat in a bar near Times Square. I had just finished performing in a musical at the Broadway Lyceum, and the producer had said that if I did not improve, he would have to replace me. My performances had deteriorated in what should have been a very popular show. The words and music just didn't seem to gel in my mind. Outside, the constant traffic swished past while neon reflections zig-zagged on the wet sidewalk. In the city that never sleeps, one particular bar looked like it had been left behind by the modern world decades ago; dark-stained furniture; dim tiffany lamps; and musty, heavy drapes. No doubt slumped on a barstool; I presented a sorry sight to the barman, a friendly guy with rimless glasses and a greying moustache.

"Hi, you from around these parts?"
I explained that I was on tour.

"What can I get you?"
I wasn't sure.

"How about a cocktail?"
I baulked at the suggestion. That was the last thing I wanted; besides, it didn't look like the sort of place that served such trendy drinks.

"What you need is an old fashioned one. Cocktails these days are a complete travesty. Fruit salad with a kick."

He took down a traditional rocks glass, put in a sugar lump moistened with Angostura Bitters, and carefully selected a chunk of ice the right size to accompany it; he then provided me with a small bar-spoon. Finally, he placed a bottle of bourbon on the bar and invited me to pour my own drink. I added what I reckoned was about the right amount, stirred it, and tasted. Oh yes, indeed, that hit the spot, and soon I was asking for another.

"Good, huh?" the barman affirmed as he served me. "It's one of the originals. Not messed about with".

The glass stood squarely on an old bar towel emblazoned with *'Buckshot Rye - Western Original'*. It was stained by rings and spills, each alluding to its own tale of inebriation. I sat there looking at them through the thick bottom of my glass.

"Folk sometimes do that with photos," I was informed. "They say they can see into a person's very soul, using the bottom of the glass as a lens."

I gazed into my glass as I stirred yet another drink and watched the swirls and blotches on the towel beneath swim before my eyes. They eventually settled, taking the form of an owl. Yes, an owl. I stared at it until it spread its wings and disappeared into the fabric. I mentioned this to the barman, who didn't seem unduly surprised.

"Perhaps you've had a little too much. Shall I phone a cab?" He was right. I was liquored up, but I knew what I saw, and it disturbed me.

"You need help," said my host. "You should talk to Cherokee Sam."

He wrote a phone number on the back of a coaster.

"Don't lose it," he said, tucking it in my top pocket as the cab arrived.

My acting and singing did not improve.

"People are paying good money to see this show," the producer remonstrated. "Go and sort yourself out while I put in your understudy, but don't take too long about it. I can't afford to carry excess baggage."

"Hello, Sam here," came a gravelly voice down the phone. "Who gave you my number?"

I couldn't remember the location of the bar or the barman's name. So I described things as best I could.

"Oh, I think you mean Mitch. There aren't many these days who know how to make a cocktail like that."

Soon, I was sitting in a small apartment in Brooklyn, listening to an elderly Native American as he helped me understand the vision I had seen in the glass.

"Do you have Native ancestors?" He asked as if he thought I had.

That was a tough one. At length, I remembered my mother saying once that my Great Grandfather was half Iroquois.

"That could account for it. It is unlikely you would have had such a vision if you did not, to some extent, share our blood. You should understand that all animals speak with one voice, in the wind, trees, moon, and sky. An owl can signify something in your life that needs attention. A new direction, perhaps. My advice is to withdraw from life for a while. Allow your spirit to observe the owl. Think carefully about what I've said.

We'll continue next week. I usually charge for a consultation, but...."

I proffered fifty dollars.

"No, I do not charge a brother."

I doubted I'd return but couldn't keep from thinking about what he'd said, so I decided to do some research.

I visited the library, watched documentaries, and searched the internet. I even took a trip to the Bronx zoo, but the owls there only blinked inscrutably.
What was I doing? I was supposed to be at the Lyceum.

"Mac's doing pretty well," said the producer. "The public loves him."
I said they could have him and walked out.

Even though I didn't think it likely, I returned to Sam's and told him about my studies.

"Try camping," he suggested.

I asked how that would help.

"The owl may find you there."

So I borrowed a tent and headed north for the Catskill Mountains.

Fall colours tinged the trees, and an earthy smell drifted from the leaf litter. I began to relax. I hadn't camped since high school. I'd forgotten how dark the night could be and was glad of my flashlight. Nothing showed up until my last night when I saw the pale form of an owl perched on an adjacent branch. It glided silently through the foliage, and I felt compelled to follow it. I was soon lost. Trying not to panic, I hunkered down until dawn when I was surprised by a woodsman who returned me to my tent.

"Be guided by the Spirit," he said.

I turned to thank him, but he had gone.

"It's time you experienced a reservation," said Sam. "I belong to the Oneida Nation. Our headquarters are here in New York City."

This puzzled me.

"No, I just happen to drive a Cherokee jeep. My daughter-in-law lives in Oneida City, about half a day's drive from here. She often takes in tourists."

Sam arranged for me to stay with her for three weeks, during which I would learn something about the Oneida way of life.

The vestiges of Iroquois in my genes may have been the reason I was drawn deeper into their culture and history. I learnt about their ethos of total community living in contrast to that of the White Man. I fell in love with a young woman called Talise, meaning Lovely Water, and having no ties elsewhere, I arranged to stay on, taking even the most menial work. In other ways, life was far from easy. Some of the young men, including a former boyfriend of Talise, took exception to me.

"You take our work and our women," they complained, trying to intimidate and goad me every chance they got.

When one of them insulted Talise, I finally snapped and was soon in a highly acrimonious brawl which left me confused and bloody.

Drums beat rhythmically in my head as two large owl eyes appeared amid chanting and whirling feathers.

When I recovered my senses, Talise was bathing my wounds.

"They're serious," she said. "You should see a doctor."

With her help and that of the local medic, my health was restored. From then on, I knew I had specific work to do on the reservation and began to look for advice on how I should proceed.

Returning one evening from a meeting in Dreamcatcher Plaza, the social hub of Oneida City, I was confronted once more by my tormenters. I braced myself for another thrashing, but to my amazement, they stopped suddenly with a look of unease, muttered something to each other, walked quickly away, and from then on respected me. I will never know quite what changed them, but on turning around, I saw an owl flying toward the darkening sky.

I attended many Oneida ceremonies and pow-wows. I even joined their language classes. This did not go unnoticed, and in due course, the elders agreed I should help teach the children their traditions, particularly as they realised I had training in the performing arts. I was honoured and enjoyed imparting to the youngsters various aspects of their heritage, encouraging them to perform traditional legends in plays, songs and dance describing their history.

During one particular session, a young boy asked me a quite unexpected question.

"What is an Eisteddfod?"

It emerged he had heard about Llangollen briefly in a news bulletin. I explained that it was a festival where different nations displayed their musical traditions.

"Wouldn't it be wonderful to take part?" he mused, at which point the other children became very excited at the prospect.

I explained it was in a country called Wales, far off in the United Kingdom, which made the practical realities of getting there quite impossible. The cost would be prohibitive. There were passports to apply for, insurance, and legal difficulties, including the hard work, needed to practice.

Undeterred, they dedicated themselves to realising their dream, the older ones supporting the younger ones. They rehearsed at every opportunity, gave concerts, and raised money any way they knew how. Their struggles to get there, and the success they had in Llangollen, is another story.

It suffices to say their achievement made a lasting impression on the whole community and beyond. Moved by such a triumph, I realised the importance of my work, which started with a vision at the bottom of a cocktail glass.

ENIGMA AND VARIATIONS

I met an old school friend in a local bar recently. I hadn't seen him for many years, and we talked for a long time, catching up on news and events. Then, after several glasses of ale, he became quiet and thoughtful. Well, we had been chin-wagging for a good while. Then he began to confide in me rather more seriously.

"John, what were your childhood holidays like?"

"Much the same as most people's, I suppose. Trips to the seaside, camping, perhaps the odd one on the continent. Why?"

He then looked very pensive. "Is there any particular one which stands out?"

I thought for a while.

"My thirteenth birthday perhaps, on holiday in Cornwall."

I proceeded to tell him how much I had enjoyed it and of the various events that made it special, but he didn't seem to be taking it in.

"Hey, are you alright?" I asked. "What is this all about?"

He then began to unfold to me an event on one such holiday that had affected the rest of his life.

"When I was about eight," he said. "My parents took me on a camping holiday in France, though I have no clear idea of the location. The weather had been rather changeable, the sea was rough, and we were all feeling rather fed up as there wasn't much to do when it was wet."

There didn't seem anything very remarkable about all this, but I let him carry on.

"One day, after a short downpour, the sun came out, and I was allowed to go to the beach, but instead, I decided to walk into the village, which, being beyond the confines of the campsite, was out of bounds. As I walked along, I came to an old, sun-bleached stone wall, with a shabby blue wooden door overhung by bougainvillaea, I think, glinting wet in the sunshine. The door was slightly ajar, and I was eaten up by curiosity to see what lay beyond it. Carefully, I pushed it open, though it gave some resistance as it didn't seem to have been used for a long time. Immediately, I was in a pine forest, with shafts of sunlight pouring through the tall trees. The delicious smell was quite intoxicating, and I was content to carry on walking over the soft, springy needles. I caught sight of a deer and decided to follow it. I eventually reached the edge of the forest, looking onto a lovely green sward. Here and there, peacocks were strutting about in front of an elegant chateau. I walked slowly up to what appeared to be the main door, and a woman came out dressed in the traditional costume of the region."

'Robin,' she cried.

"Hearing my name called instantly made me feel that somehow I belonged there."

'It's been so long. How lovely to see you.'

"She gave me a big hug. I'd never met such a kindly, warm-hearted person. She invited me inside and, with some other children, gave me a wonderful lunch. After, she showed me a beautiful garden. A cloud of white doves rose up onto the rooftops. There were bright butterflies, and the scent of lavender and roses seemed to pervade the garden. Small monkeys scampered in the trees, and glittering hummingbirds darted among the fuchsia and hibiscus blooms. I played there happily all afternoon with my newfound friends until, eventually, it occurred to me that my parents must be getting worried as to my whereabouts. So, very reluctantly, I decided to leave as quickly as possible before getting into too much trouble."

'Leaving so soon?' said the good lady. 'But you must stay a few days.'

"The thought of spending the rest of my holiday there was very attractive. I had been so happy, but I insisted I could stay no longer. The shadows were lengthening, and I was wondering if I could remember my way back. The lady looked very dejected but, with a deep sigh, said she understood. She took me to a door in the courtyard, opened it, and let me through, not without a hug and a wave.

To my surprise, I was standing just outside the campsite, and when I looked back, the door and the chateau had gone, leaving only bracken in its place. I ran back to my parents, apologising for being so long, but they seemed rather nonplussed."

'Aren't you going to the beach?" said my mother. "Lunch won't be for another hour.'

"It seemed I had been away only a few minutes. I knew there was no use explaining my adventure, so I

110

kept this experience to myself until now. You are the only person I have ever told."

I felt strangely privileged to hear my friend's story. It seemed quite unbelievable, but he insisted it was true.

"For years, I have racked my brains trying to remember the spot and have been to France several times to try and find the blue door again in that sun-bleached stone wall, but it has always eluded me. On one occasion, I went with my wife and family to Brittany and thought I had found it, but the door led into a run-down courtyard with old farming equipment. Another time we went to the Loire district, and I found a door that could be the one, but on opening, I found it led into a private garden, where a startled old lady, in no uncertain manner, made sure I made a swift exit.

The last time, I was on my own. My father had recently passed away, and I was taking time out to think things over. I was staying in self-catering accommodation southwest of Bordeaux, and this time I truly thought I had found it. I approached the door, full of anticipation, my mind racing. I could almost smell the pine trees as I began to open it, but there was only a field of maize beyond.

Now my children have grown up, and I live alone. My hopes of finding that wonderful place again are completely spent, and I know I will never return there."

He seemed very downcast and lonely. I felt sorry for him, so a couple of days ago I decided to pay him a visit. After several attempts at the doorbell and getting no reply, I looked through his lounge window and saw him sitting in an armchair. So I called on a neighbour, who fortunately had a key.

"It's me, John!" I called as I entered the hallway.

My friend took no notice and seemed absorbed in poring over a holiday brochure. The page open before him showed a door very like the one he had described. It was accompanied by pictures of a chateau with beautiful gardens set in a pine forest. He did not seem to notice me even then, so intent was he in his deliberation. I spoke his name.

"Robin, are you alright?"

I touched him but, to my great dismay, found he was dead. And the paradise he was searching for? Who knows the truth of it?

THE FALL: A WINTER'S SAGA

In an age gone by, the northern tribes spent the long winter nights beside blazing fires. They whittled logs into fantastic creations and told tales of life in the mists bordering reality. Youngsters would be spellbound; adults attentive, and old folk would drift in and out of dreams.

The tradition in these northern lands was for people to sit around and listen to a tale from their best storyteller while winter storms besieged their longhouse.

On such a night, when the dancing flames imbue branches with wild and even malicious life, a knock is heard. One of the men picks up a weapon and slowly draws back the great wooden bolt. A writhing blizzard of snow roars through the open doorway, but there is nobody outside. Two strong guards put their shoulders to the door, driving the elements back into the darkness. But someone has entered unseen under the cloak of the tempest, for there in the middle of the room stands a figure, tall, thin, wizened and gnarled, looking for all the world as if he could break in two like a dry stick. His long red hair and beard mingle with his tattered yellow and green clothes that reach his toes. He is indeed a curious sight.

An age seems to pass until the chief finally speaks.

"You are welcome, friend. Warm yourself and share our table."

Their guest says nothing but moves to the midst of their company. He holds out a long staff carved with ancient runic symbols. He points it at people, fixing them with a piercing stare, kindling fear in his wake as he turns from one to the other. He continues, gyrating, slowly at first, then with increased speed. His hair and clothes fly out around him in an increasingly bizarre swirl of colour and energy. Giddy with watching, the onlookers gasp as he rises into the air. The roof breaks open. He mounts a white horse in the sky and vanishes.

Torteg opened his eyes and looked around at his companions lying about in a meadow, where their livestock quietly grazed sweet spring grass. Nearby gushed a river swollen by melting snow from distant mountains above the forested hillside.

Others were beginning to wake and, like him, rubbed their eyes with astonishment. The elders gathered to discuss what was to be done. Everyone could remember the strange character that had transfixed them all.

Torteg walked across to where Marika was attending to her father.

"Where do you suppose we are?"

"Who knows?" She said. "More importantly, how do we get home?"

He was at a loss to answer her. This didn't seem such a bad place to settle if they had to. Marika, however, wary of dangers that may lurk, was not so sure. Anyway, there were things she missed from their home. Torteg, however, was her man. She was carrying his child and would follow him where ever he went.

A murmur came from the council. The one person missing was Griffic, the storyteller.

"That stranger was a wight," said one. "The door should never have been opened."

"Too late, Vitec," said another.

They could see a castle not too far away, approached by a winding track. An agreement was reached to send a delegation to find out where they were and if there was shelter to be had.

"Careful, Torteg," said Marika as he joined the band that began to make its way up the hill.

On reaching the fortification, Fitog, the chief, knocked boldly on the door. There was no answer. He pushed the door and found it began to give way. Aided by two burly men, the heavy, wooden structure eventually yielded and opened into a great hall that was obviously used for assemblies and feasting. Still, nobody came.

"We come in peace," cried Fitog, but the silence pressed in from all sides.

They decided they should separate into pairs to explore the castle and arranged to meet back in the hall. Torteg and his companion mounted a flight of stairs. Hearing a noise behind a closed door, they cautiously opened it. With a clatter of wings, a flock of starlings took flight through a small window, leaving silence.

The place was deserted, and from the lookout tower, there was no other evidence of human habitation nearby. They agreed to spend the night there, taking turns to keep watch. No sound or movement disturbed their slumbers. After several further nights, when no intruders claimed it as their own, Fitog declared:

"This castle is ours, and we shall defend it."

Torteg was dispatched along with two companions to lead the community to their new home.

Years rolled by, and the company thrived. They tilled the fertile land: reared their livestock, and lived off the bounty provided by the river and forest.

After several years of peaceful rule, Fitog died, and Karon took over as chief, but he did not have the charisma and respect his predecessor had. Many disliked him, causing dissent among the people, which grew until, eventually, the whole community split into two factions. Karon still ruled from the castle, but the dissenters lived in longhouses close by.

Families were split in the feuding, and while Torteg still owed allegiance to the chief, his son sided with the rebels. At length, the dissenters planned a bold attack. Rain and thunder raged around as they crept towards the castle, fleetingly accentuated by flashes of lightning. A spy, however, had informed Karon of their approach, and his men were ready for them.

The two parties exploded into a bloody battle in which death reigned over both sides. Torteg faced his son. Weapons ready, each waiting for the other to make a move. Amid the battle's chaos, a flash of lightning picked out a figure scrutinising them from a white horse on the hillside and at once, all fell dark and silent.

"And so," Griffic says. "That is the legend of our ancestors."

The storm has abated; the fire is hot, and the rough brew has had its effect. Karon quietly sits with Fitog and his men, all silent in their own thoughts, while his mother helps the other women prepare their children for sleep. Torteg lies by Marika, who is pregnant with their first child, and Fitog sits in thoughtful silence. The pensive atmosphere, broken only by the occasional whimper of an infant, grips them all. Each knows what the other dare not tell.

UNCLE BORIS'S SECRET FORMULA

"Wow! It must be the biggest pumpkin in the world," said Jasper.

"Well, I don't know about that," said Uncle Boris, "but it's certainly the biggest on the allotment. I'm expecting it to win at the Autumn Produce Show. Here you see months of careful nurturing, watering, and feeding."

"Feeding?" said Jasper.

"Oh yes", said Uncle Boris, "plenty of manure and," he whispered, "a few drops daily of my secret formula." He revealed a sauce bottle containing a treacly liquid labelled SECRET FORMULA: USE WITH CARE.

"What's in it?" Jasper asked.

"Ah, now that's my secret," said Uncle Boris.

The idea of a secret formula was very exciting. His friends gasped in amazement as Jasper described the pumpkin, except for one.

"Huh, my Grandad's pumpkin is much bigger than that, and it's going to win the prize for sure."

"Oh yeah?" said Jasper. "We'll see about that,"

Tommy Riley always had to go one better. Well, not this time.

Back at the allotment, Jasper thought of the wonderful Halloween lantern the pumpkin would make. He couldn't bear the thought of another bigger than it.

"Don't worry," said Boris. "With my formula, it will be big enough when the time comes."

"Couldn't you give it a bit extra, just to make sure?" said Jasper.

Uncle Boris, however, was quite confident. Anyway, the show was not for another three weeks, so perhaps he was right.

Every day the pumpkin grew a little larger, and every day Tommy Riley said:

"My Grandad's is bigger."

When the day of the show arrived, Uncle Boris's pumpkin was quite a monster. Jasper proudly watched him place it on the table with the other entries making his misgivings seem quite foolish. It was bound to win, but where was the one that Tommy's Grandad was entering?

"Where's your Grandad's pumpkin?" Jasper asked Tommy.

"He's bringing it soon, and he will put it right next to your Uncle's so everyone can see it's the biggest."

Jasper's doubts returned. He had to do something and ran to the allotment. Taking the key to the shed from under a flower pot, he went inside. Eventually, he saw what he wanted on a high shelf and, standing on a rickety chair, just managed to reach it.

Jasper hurried back to the vegetable marquee in time to hear an official ask everyone to leave while the judging took place.

"Come on, Tommy. We must go now," called a man heading for the exit, expecting his grandson to follow him.

Few noticed a small boy slip under the rope and pour the entire contents of a sauce bottle over his Uncle's pumpkin.

"Ok, Tommy Riley," he said to himself. "No contest."

Soon, outside, people began staring at the vegetable tent. As they seemed to be waiting for the result, Jasper turned confidently with them to hear the judge's decision.

There was a strange ripping and creaking noise, and to Jasper's horror, the marquee was slowly bulging. Tables and produce were thrust outside as the canvas tore alarmingly. The thing grew steadily bigger until finally, there, higher than the trees, was the biggest pumpkin in the world.

"Help!" cried Tommy from the top.

It was obvious now; he had been bluffing all the time.

"Oh, oh!" Jasper groaned.

Uncle Boris stood nearby, and he did not look amused.

"I think we should call the fire brigade, don't you, Jasper?"

Christmas

THE UNFINISHED SHEPHERD

The woodcarver sat in his armchair beside the fire, reading a newspaper. Slowly he turned a page.

"Well, Tiger," he said to the ginger cat lying contentedly on his lap, "Christmas is drawing on."

He was looking at a colourful advertisement with lanterns, stars, and a big Santa Claus. It announced a Grand Christmas Fair at the local market.

"What shall I do for the fair, Tiger?"

He thought for a while.

"Perhaps I will carve a set of nativity figures to sell. You know, Mary, Joseph, and the Child Jesus in the manger, and so on. But I won't make them very big, or they'll not be finished in time. Mm, I must see what wood I have in stock."

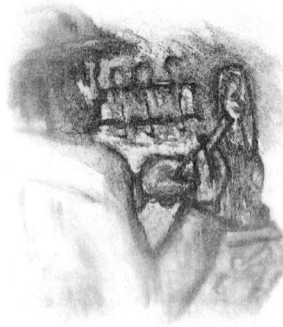

The next day he went to his store, where he examined a few logs.

"They're too big," he sighed. "I am only making small figures such as would fit on a mantelpiece."

Then he took out a branch that he had cut from the old pear tree in his garden and which had been seasoning for several years.

"Ah, this is better. My pear tree is too old to produce much fruit, but it does provide shelter for the wildlife, and now it will produce fruit of a different kind."

He took it back to his shed, got out his carving tools, and shaved the branch about six inches from the end. He decided to make a shepherd first to be sure of his technique before he carved the Holy Family. He outlined the head and body, indicating the robes, and then refined the details. It took a couple of hours, but after the final smoothing with sandpaper, there stood a little shepherd.

"It could be better," he said to himself, "but it's ok. I must press on with the others if I am to be ready for the fair."

Next, he carved Mary, Joseph, and the manger with the Christ Child. Satisfied, he put them next to the shepherd.

"I could do with another shepherd now," he thought out loud. "One with a lamb in his arms, perhaps."

He took the branch again, shorter now after cutting the other figures, and shaved it as before. Again, he outlined the main details and began to refine them, but try as he might, he could not get it right. He persevered, using various knives and gouges, but they didn't seem to cut properly. He thought perhaps they weren't sharp enough, so he honed the blades on his stones and polished them on his leather strop until they were razor-sharp, but he still could not cut the wood as he wanted; in fact, the piece was ruined. "Oh dear," he murmured. "I really can't afford to spend any more time on this one." So, regretfully, he cut it off from the branch, and the little figure fell to the floor of the shed among all the debris of wood shavings, sawdust, and scraps of used sandpaper.

The woodcarver started work on another shepherd, and when it was successfully completed, he made some sheep, an ox, and an ass. Next, he carved three wise men and even a camel. Pleased with them, he bought some coloured polish to finish the figures, and he thought it would be a good idea to try it on a spare piece of wood so that if he didn't like the effect, the figures would not be spoilt. At that moment, he thought of the unfinished shepherd lying on the floor of the shed.

"I'll try that," he thought, "if I can find it."

Surprisingly enough, it was quite easy to find. He squeezed some polish from its tube on a piece of rag, and rubbed it over the little figure, then buffed it with a soft cloth, giving the wood a beautiful sheen of terracotta red, highlighting the natural grain.

"That will do," he said to himself and popped the unfinished shepherd into his pocket.

Using the same lovely colour, he polished all the figures, giving them a warm glow. Now, all that was needed was a stable. So he set about making a little rood shelter for them with two lengths of knotty oak, a flat piece of wood for the floor, and another for the roof, which he covered with bark. When it was finished, he arranged his figures in it and stood back to see how they looked.

"They don't look too bad, but it isn't quite complete; there's something missing, and I can't quite think what it is. Anyway, I haven't got time to carve any more now. I must take them to the fair tomorrow,"

He fingered the unfinished shepherd in his pocket, took it out and looked at it thoughtfully.

"Mm, I wonder...."

The next morning, the woodcarver took his crib to the Christmas fair and set it out on a stall along with other seasonal craft items. Passers-by often stopped to look at it. Some even picked up the figures and examined them. One lady said she would love to buy them, but she had to see to her family's needs and didn't think she would be able to afford the crib as well.

"Strange," thought the woodcarver, "that a tableau reminding people of the poverty of Christ should itself be a luxury."

The day wore on, and finally, the stall-holders began to pack up. The woodcarver hadn't sold his crib, so he packed up too.

"Never mind," he said to himself, rather disappointed. "I will have to sell it elsewhere. Perhaps my friend who runs a gift shop could sell it for me."

The following Sunday was the first one of Advent. The theme was preparation, and children were buying Advent calendars at the back of the church. Unable to wait until they got home, some were excitedly opening the first window, which revealed an angel.

At once, he realised that was what he needed to complete his crib.

"But unfortunately," he sighed, "the branch is finished, and it would look odd if I used a different piece of wood."

He put his hand into his pocket to take some money out for the collection at the door and felt the unfinished shepherd. He drew it out and looked at it.

"What have you got there?" asked some friends.

"It's an unfinished shepherd," said the woodcarver. "It was going to be part of a crib I've made, but it went wrong."

"What a shame," one of them said. "He can go in my crib any time."

Another said: "What will you do with it?"

"I think, I think, "the woodcarver said, "I think I will turn it into an angel."

When he got home, he took the unfinished shepherd and, selecting a V tool, cut a deep furrow down the middle of its back; then, he carved the two halves into a pair of wings. He refined the head and carved the robes so they flowed as if the angel was in flight, then renewed its terracotta polish. Finally, he screwed a small hook in the shoulders so that it could be suspended from a little screw-eye in the roof of the stable. Sitting back in his chair, he surveyed his work. The ginger cat jumped on his lap, and he stroked its warm fur.

"Well, Tiger, my crib is complete now, but who will buy it?"

A few days later, the woodcarver was attending a carol concert in aid of a local charity when he felt a touch on his arm.

"Didn't I see you at the fair?" It was the lady who had wanted to buy his crib. "I don't suppose you still have the Nativity set you were selling, do you?"

"Yes, I have," he answered.

"Oh, I'm so pleased," she said happily. "I was afraid you may have sold it."

"No, no, it's still there."

"I would very much like to buy it;" and so saying, she paid the woodcarver then and there.

When he delivered it to her door the next day, she invited him in for a glass of sherry and a mince pie. He watched her set the little figures out on the window sill and was pleased they had found a good home.

"That's an ideal place for them," she said as he left. "They can be seen nicely there."

Finally, at midnight on Christmas Eve, the lady quietly slipped the manger with the infant Jesus between Mary and Joseph. Far off in the still night, a church bell rang. Then softly, softly, the snow began to fall. The first delicate flakes, upon touching the ground, melted away in seconds, yet soon everything was clothed in pure white, as in renewed innocence. Reflected by the snow, the moon filled the little stable with a wonderful light, and from his place in the roof, the angel, no longer an unfinished shepherd, kept watch over the Holy Family. From somewhere in the house, the carol of Silent Night could be heard, sung in the clear voice of a single choir boy. Christmas had come at last. Hope was rekindled, and the Christ Child was born once more in the hearts of believers.

THE SNOW GLOBE

He's growing up fast, my grandson. Six years old now and bright as a button. I'd come to visit my family for the holidays and brought him a copy of a Christmas picture book I'd been commissioned to illustrate earlier that year. He loved it and even took it to bed. He was still looking at it when I went up to say goodnight, and he said thoughtfully.

"Grandad, how did you get to be an artist?"

"Well, Terry," I answered, pulling up a chair, "I've always enjoyed painting and drawing, just like you, but when I was your age, colours were very expensive. Although I dearly wanted a box of paints for Christmas, I knew my parents could not easily afford them."

"You could have written a letter to Father Christmas like I did."

"It's a good idea, Terry, and that's exactly what I did. I wrote my letter as carefully as I could and left it by the fireplace where he would be sure to find it. I soon forgot all about it, though, because there was a ring at the doorbell, and in walked Uncle Fabian, come to stay for the holidays. My little brother and I were thrilled.

I don't know what it was about him, but there always seemed a kind of magic in the air when he was around. Anything could happen. One Christmas Eve, when he was with us, I can't have been any older than you and my brother a couple of years younger; we were looking out for some sign of Santa's arrival. The frosty air seemed filled with the faint sound of sleigh bells, and my brother was sure he saw a flash in the sky headed by a red light."

"No kidding? Really?"

"Who knows what he saw? Now, where was I?"

"You had written a letter to Father Christmas, and then Uncle Fabian came."

"Ah, yes, as I said, he was special. We could hardly wait for him to take his coat off. We followed him into the living room, and, finally, he put his hand into a battered old shopping bag. For my brother, he drew out a toy monkey that did tricks on a stick. I haven't seen one of those for ages. To me, however, he gave a snow globe."

"What's a snow globe?"

"It's a glass ball, often containing a Christmassy scene, and when you turn it over and back, little snowflakes swirl and tumble around inside."

"I'd like one of those," said Terry.

"Well. I'd never seen anything so beautiful and was completely enchanted by it. It contained a snowman, a Christmas tree, and Father Christmas on his sleigh flying in a midnight blue sky, and I never tired of gazing into it as the little snowflakes fell.

The next morning, the snow really did fall heavily, and that afternoon my brother and I ran out into the back garden to make a snowman. We worked hard, rolling and piling the snow until we had a good shape. We used coal for his eyes and buttons, a carrot for his nose, and put an old scarf around him to keep him warm. I then decided he needed a pipe. My brother said he was sure he'd seen one and ran indoors, emerging some minutes later with an old briar pipe which we triumphantly put in the mouth of our creation."

"I wish it would snow here," said Terry. "So as I can make a snowman too."

I gave a little sigh.

"I'm sure you do, but I hope it waits 'till I get back home."

"Go on, go on; what happened next?"

"It was getting dark by this time, but before going indoors, we turned and looked at our work. It was just as in my snow globe, except the snowman in there didn't have a pipe, but the old fir tree in our garden stood in very nicely as the Christmas tree. All it needed now was Father Christmas in his sleigh.

As we made our way towards the house, we found our way was blocked by something almost like glass, from which it was impossible to break free."

'We're inside the snow globe,' said my brother.

'Looks like it,' I admitted, though I couldn't see how.

We saw our mother open the back door and throw some scraps out for the birds.

We shouted and hammered as loudly and as hard as we could, but it made no difference; she didn't even seem to notice us."

"Weren't you frightened?" asked Terry.

"Indeed we were. Both of us were cold and scared, while my brother became tearful as snow began to fall.

"Don't cry," I said. "We'll find a way out. Let's shelter under the tree. "

The fir branches reached right to the ground. So, wondering how in the world we could escape, we crept underneath them. We couldn't have been there more than a few minutes when there was a loud swishing sound, the jingle of bells, and crunch of hooves in the snow, along with a strong animal smell. Together we looked cautiously out, and to our amazement, we saw a large red sleigh with a team of snorting reindeer, their warm breath steaming as it rose in the freezing air. An old man with a white beard sat in the driving seat. He was dressed in a red cloak trimmed with white fur.

'It's Father Christmas,' whispered my brother in great awe."

"I knew it! I knew it!" shouted Terry excitedly.

"I also was in no doubt as to who it was, but I fancied I recognised a more familiar person in the old man's face. We gaped in wonder at the whole spectacle, glowing with hundreds of fairy lights and jingling with little bells. The man laughed in a jolly kind of way and handed us each a parcel with our name on the label. Before we could say anything, he shook the reins, urging his team forward.

With more laughter and a cry of 'A Merry Christmas to all, and to all a good night,' the sleigh sped into the sky.

Just as it reached the point where it was in the snow globe, the barrier burst like a bubble, and our mother came out to bring us in for tea. As we went in with her, we turned for a final look. There was the fir tree and our snowman, but no sign of Father Christmas, not even hoof prints in the snow. And that, you might think, is the end of the story."

"Isn't it, Grandad? It was just a dream, wasn't it?" said young Terry.

"Well, I might have thought so myself if it wasn't for the presents. Another curious thing, though. The next morning, Uncle Fabian was looking for his pipe. Sure that it must be the one we'd used for the snowman, I ran out to get it, The thaw in the night had left behind the bits and pieces we had used for him, but no matter how hard I looked, I couldn't find the pipe.

At that moment, with shouts of excitement, my brother ran out with my snow globe.

'Look, look,' he shouted, 'he's got the pipe. The snowman's got the pipe.'

And sure enough, the snowman was now sporting a little briar pipe where there hadn't been one before."

"Is that true, Grandad?" said Terry wonderingly.

"What do you think? Here, I'll show you."

I took the little snow globe from my pocket and held it for Terry to see.

"Look, I've kept it all these years."

"Grandad, the snowman really has got a pipe!" he said in amazement. "But, there is still one thing; what was in the parcels?"

"I thought perhaps you had forgotten about them."

"No, no. you've got to finish the story."

"OK. Everyone was very surprised on Christmas day when we opened these presents, except perhaps for Uncle Fabian. My brother had a beautiful Noah's Ark set, complete with Noah and his family, all the animals in twos, and of course, the boat itself.

"What happened to your brother, Grandad?"

"Oh, he became a vet and eventually settled in New Zealand."

"Your present, Grandad? What was in your present?"

"You know, I couldn't believe it as I opened the most beautiful box of paints I had ever seen. The colours were so bright."

"Is that what made you an artist?"

"It's certainly what started me off, but it took many years of training, practice, and hard work before I could earn my living as one."

Finally, I turned my snow globe, and Terry watched the little flakes float down over the snowman, the Christmas tree, and even Father Christmas. I left it by his bed as my grandson snuggled down under his duvet. In the soft glow of the nightlight, he was soon in the land of Nod. I quietly slipped out, thinking of the time Uncle Fabian gave me the snow globe. Hm; to me, it was always magical.

THE LONELY SNOWFLAKE

The snowfall that Christmas was more than usual. It lay until well after January when people began to complain about how cold it was, how it was bad for business and bad for health. But the children enjoyed playing in a world many of them had only seen on Christmas cards. By Candlemas, the snow was starting to look a bit jaded, and even the youngsters began to tire of it. At last, a welcome thaw began to expose familiar surroundings in their stark reality as the ice melted away. Patches persisted in a few sheltered places, some of them as strange grey piles that used to be snowmen.

During the festive season, a Christmas tree, erected in aid of a local charity, had stood in the town square. Now, its lights and all the decorations had been packed away until the following December. A cold wind blew as the volunteers worked, and they did not notice a little snowflake blow from the tree, flutter off into the park, and come to rest on a small patch of snow.

The snowflake lay with others, packed together in a little white clump, but eventually, the clouds parted, allowing the sun to gently warm the frozen ground. At this, all the snowflakes embraced each other and began to melt away. The snowflake from the Christmas tree wanted to join them but try as it might to melt, it was soon left alone on the bare earth.

Its sparkle attracted a foraging magpie, which came over and pecked at it.

"What's this?"

"I'm a snowflake."

"Why are you here alone? You should be melting with your friends."

"I don't know. The wind blew me here, but I wish I could melt with the others."

"Never mind; you'll make a fine addition to my collection."

So saying, the magpie picked it up and took it to her nest in an old oak tree.

The snowflake joined a diverse assembly of found objects. There were pieces of glass, bottle tops, pebbles, shiny buttons, and even a diamond ring, but although these were all very attractive, the snowflake felt alone and longed to melt like the others.

Somehow, the wise old oak tree sensed its sorrow.

"What's the matter, little snowflake? Why are you so unhappy?"

"I do so want to melt away with my friends, but here I am, alone and as hard as ever. Why am I different? How is it they can melt and not me?"

"They melt because of love."

"Love, what is that, and how can it make them melt?" asked the snowflake.

"It is a fire that warms their hearts until finally, they give themselves to each other so completely that they melt together and are able to do wonderful things."

"What sort of wonderful things?"

"They turn to water as you see," said the oak tree. "Then run into the ground and feed all the plants, like the winter pansies in the flower bed there, and even big trees like myself."

"How can I find this love?"

"That I cannot answer, but I think if you want it badly enough, it will find you."

Spring came early, and from its place in the tree, the snowflake watched the snowdrops bloom and fade away back into the earth. Later, some trees nearby burst into white blossom. A strong wind came and blew the petals from the branches, along with the snowflake from the magpie's nest, and they blew like a blizzard, forming delicate little drifts. But eventually, the petals too faded into the ground leaving the snowflake from the Christmas tree alone and forgotten once more.

Spring gave way to summer, and some small children came to play in the park, enjoying the fine weather. One of them shouted to her friends.

"Look what I've found."

The others ran to see what it was and saw the little snowflake glinting in the sunshine. A little girl took it to show her mother.

"Can we keep it to put on our Christmas tree?"

The woman looked in surprise at the rather weathered snowflake.

"No, dear, it's very dirty. We can't have that in the house. Let's put it in the bin on our way home."

The little girl wrinkled up her face and began to protest.

"Don't cry, dear; I'm sure Daddy will get us lots of lovely new snowflakes for our Christmas tree nearer the time."

This seemed to pacify her, and as they came to the park gates, she popped it in the recycling bin.

The snowflake lay there amongst all sorts of plastic rubbish; picnic refuse, carrier bags, broken toys, bottles and containers of every description, none of which seemed very pleasant. The snowflake felt miserable. How was it to find love here? It wished it was back with the old oak tree and thought of what it had said.

One day the bin was emptied into a truck collecting plastic. The waste was eventually tipped into a larger container, and soon the snowflake began to feel warmer. The heat became so intense that it was afraid it would burn up altogether. It looked around at its companions, who had seemed unattractive and found a love for them growing within.

Soon it began to embrace them. Giving itself freely to all the other bits of plastic as they melted and became one with them. At last, disregarding the pain, the snowflake was blissfully happy, having achieved its desire.

The molten plastic, on cooling, was made into useful objects, and the snowflake became part of a plastic cup, which, along with hundreds of others, was packed up and sold.

In a city many miles away, a man with his heavily pregnant wife took refuge for the night in a garage because all the accommodation was filled by people that had come for a festival.

The woman cried out in the pangs of labour while the man stood by encouraging her and helping where he could. When the child was finally born, he wrapped it in a towel and laid the infant in a packing case full of shredded paper. Next, the man brought some instant soup in a plastic cup from a hot drinks machine that the mechanics used. It warmed the woman, and her strength began to return as she sipped the comforting broth from the cup. The snowflake felt happy to play some small part in giving aid to the mother, and when she finished the soup, the cup was ready to be melted and moulded again, perhaps into Christmas snowflakes.

SEASONAL SPROUTS

One December morning, Mr Grumble trudged into his garden to pick sprouts from his vegetable patch, but to his horror, he saw the best ones had gone. He surveyed the cloven hoof prints all around in the virgin snow and hurried back indoors to tell his wife.

"This is the devil's work. He's trying to ruin our Christmas."

"Oh, don't be daft, Dan. It's quite obvious they're being eaten by some animal. Probably a goat or something that had got away from Fiddlers Farm. I'll give them a ring to see if any of their animals are missing."

Betty, the farmer's wife, consulted her husband, but the livestock were all safe and warm in their various stalls.

"Vera, Vera," shouted Dan from the back door. "I can hear something moving around in the summer house. I'm not going in there on my own. I'm getting Bert to bring his gun."

"You're a big scaredy-cat," she replied. "I'll show you what this thing is."

So saying, she put on her gumboots and made her way along where she reckoned the garden path was, towards the wooden chalet that had never looked less like a summer house. She had almost reached the half-open door when a wail stopped her in her tracks.

"It sounds a bit like a cat," said Mrs Grumble, "but I've never heard a cat quite like that. You may be right. I

141

don't think it is very safe to go in there. What shall we do?"

"I may be able to see something through the window," answered Dan. "Then, at least, we will know what we're dealing with."

He crept towards the summer house. Peeking through the door as he went but couldn't see anything. He wiped away the frost from a window to have a better look. The noise came again, and he bolted back to where his wife was standing.

"Well?" she said.

"I couldn't see anything. It was too dark."

"Oh, you're hopeless. If you can't deal with it, the only thing to do is to call the police."

"No, no. You remember when we thought we had an intruder; those policemen trampled all over my strawberries. I'm not making that mistake again."

"You didn't help by hovering around behind them."

"I'm getting Bert," Mr Grumble persisted. "He belongs to a gun club. We'll sort this out together."

His wife sighed in exasperation.

"Oh, heaven help us! You couldn't knock the skin off a rice pudding, the pair of you. I'm busy defrosting the fridge," and she returned indoors to a more controlled chill.

Dan and Bert decided the best thing to do was to erect a hide, from which they could watch for whatever was in the summer-house to appear. They soon constructed a rough screen from bean poles and conifer

142

branches, then settled down with flasks of hot, strong coffee.

Dan took a sip from his steaming beverage.

"Keep your pistol trained, Bert. We'll get it as soon as it comes out."

As the daylight began to fail, Bert could endure it no longer. In spite of his thermals, the biting cold had entered the very marrow of his bones.

"Are you sure there's something in there?" he said.

"Positive. A big cat or some such creature. I heard it myself."

"Well, I don't know about you, but I'm perished out here. Let's go in for a warm."

Mrs Grumble laid a trail of newspapers for them to walk on.

"Take off your boots," she said. "Have you got it yet?"

"No, It's staying put." Dan groused. "We'll have to think of another strategy."

Bert grunted.

"I don't know," said Mrs Grumble. "A right pair of huntsmen you make. Stay in here while I clean the lounge."

With better things to do, she left them in the kitchen, hugging the warm stove. Dan had just poured a couple of scotches when they heard her calling.

"Dan, Dan, come quickly. It's coming out!"

The two friends trooped into the lounge, and in the dusk, through the French windows, they saw a deer hesitantly stepping from the summer house. Dan gasped.

"So that's what's been eating my sprouts. I wouldn't mind a bit of venison for Christmas. How about you, Bert? I'll have my sprouts one way or another. Hurry!"

At that moment, a plane passed low over the rooftops, and the deer vanished back inside its refuge. Dan swore.

"Let's finish our scotch and go out again." They sipped their drinks.   The deer began to emerge once more.

"Get your revolver ready, Bert. We'll have it this time."

"That you won't." Mrs Grumble intervened as a small fawn tentatively followed its mother.

"Well, I'll be damned!" said Bert.

"Those two have taken shelter from the weather in our garden," said Mrs Grumble. "Look how the mother is showing the littl'n where to feed."

"Yes, on my sprouts!"

"You leave them alone. They trust us, and I won't have that betrayed. You harm them, Mr Grumble, and I'll never speak to you again."

"Ahh, Dan," Bert added. "How can you think of such a thing? Look at them."

Outnumbered, Dan's heart melted.

"You're right. They may as well enjoy a Christmas dinner too. Heaven knows the weather's cold enough."

"It's started snowing again," said Mrs Grumble drawing the curtains.

"Do you think we could charge people to see them?" Dan asked his wife.

She shot him a look that made him wince, then switched on the television.

Early the next morning, two shadows stole from the summer house of number 26 Oakland Road, leaving two tracks across the snowy field at the back of the garden toward the woodland beyond.

PUNCH'S CHRISTMAS CRACKER

It all kicked off about a week before Christmas. Judy was busy downstairs. It's best to keep out of her way when she's in that mood. I was reading a newspaper to see if I was in it. There's always someone who objects to my way of life, but they can't get rid of me that easily. I've survived more than three hundred and fifty years. I'm still here, though, still kicking, and I still have a big following.

"Mr Punch! Mr Punch, come and help me," shouted Judy from downstairs.

So, of course, I went to see what was wrong and found her shampooing and hoovering the carpet, but she'd accidentally hoovered up the baby. What a state she was in, and the baby too. I pulled him from the bag, and Judy held him while I vacuumed all the duff and flust from him. Then she had the cheek to say:

"Do something useful and look after him."

She put him to bed and told me to sing him a lullaby saying:

"He'll go right off."

So I tried 'Rock-a-Bye Baby' in my best singing voice. Unfortunately, it was me that nodded off instead, and when I woke up, the little tyke had legged it. Ooh! Judy was cross.

"You told me he'd go right off," I said, but that didn't cut much ice.

"I'm having a bake-off," she said, "and I'm starting with you." At which she took a swipe at me with her rolling pin.

I needed no further encouragement and hot-footed it to the Red Lion.

"And while you're out, you can get me a box of crackers for…," Judy bawled after me.

I was well down the street by then, so I didn't quite catch the last word. Was it Christmas?

I met Joey the Clown, well ensconced at the bar, with his dog Toby.

"Hello, Mr Punch," he said. "What brings you here?"

"Keeping out of Judy's way. She's in a filthy temper."

"What's wrong?"

"Baby's gone missing. It's not my fault. Anyway, he's bound to turn up again soon, like a bad penny."

I ordered a pint of ale and some pork scratchings. Toby's very partial to pork scratchings, and as I was about to eat one, he jumped up at me, and I spilt my drink. Now, this was serious. You can't come between a man and his ale, so I warned him that if he did it again, I'd have to take action. Well, no sooner had I bought another drink than he was at it again.

"Go on; give him a scratching," said Joey.

"Not likely," I said. "Your dog's a little so-n-so. He's getting more than a scratching." I raised my stick to give him what for, but before I could say, "That's the way to do it," he'd grabbed hold of it with his teeth and wouldn't let go.

"Let go," I said, "let go!"

The harder I pulled, the more he pulled. Back and forth we went until finally he DID let go, and I toppled backwards right off my bar stool. Joey couldn't contain himself for laughing.

At that moment, P.C Bobby walked in.

"Hello, hello, hello. Why aren't you out looking for your baby?"

"That's your job," I replied. "How am I supposed to know where he is?"

"I'll deal with you later," said the policeman, grumbling, as he walked out. "It's perishing cold out there."

Funny how, wrapped in his great overcoat, he reminded me of something wrapped in bacon I hoped to have with my Christmas dinner. Toby ran after him, jumping up, growling, and barking. Little did P.C. Bobby know I'd slipped a pork scratching in his coat pocket.

"I'd better be going. Judy wants some crackers." I said, alighting from my perch.

Joey grinned and offered me a box of beautiful red ones. "Here, take these as a Christmas present."

"Thanks, Joey. Much obliged. Here, have a drink on me," and I bought him a pint of the best stout.

Back home, Judy was still not happy.

"Not those," she yelled. "I said crackers for cheese."

So that was the bit I'd missed.

"Come on, Judy," I suggested. "Let's make up and pull one."

We did, and surprise! Surprise! With a loud snap, out popped the baby. Well, she was that happy she hugged me, kissed me, and told me how clever I was (which I always knew). So, it looked like we might have a jovial Christmas after all. It just remains for me to wish all my friends the compliments of the Season. So long.

THE CAROL SINGERS

Heather, her younger sister Molly, and their little brother Timmy stood before the gates of an old manor. A light burned in an upper window, accentuating the evening gloom. Trees, like crazy wrought ironwork, lined a winding driveway.

"We're lost, aren't we, Heather? I knew we shouldn't have come carol singing."

"We had to get out of the house, Molly. Mum and Dad were having a terrible row. They're getting worse."

"Can't we go home?" said Timmy. "I don't like it here. It looks like the witch's house..."

"No, there's no witch." Heather cleared her throat. "We'll sing some carols and ask for help."

The gate creaked, and they crept down the dark avenue. Heather was trying to ignore the churning in her stomach as snow dripped from the bare branches.

"I've heard she traps people and turns them to stone or something," said Molly.

"I want to go home," Timmy whimpered. He was about to bolt, but Heather grabbed him by the hood of his parka.

"That's enough from both of you."

The path led to an imposing doorway. Heather lifted a heavy knocker, which reverberated around the cavernous porch. More to keep up their spirits than anything else, she suggested singing 'Away in a Manger.' They raised querulous voices to the familiar tune and words. Nobody came. 'Jingle Bells' was next, but with little enthusiasm. Then, slowly, the big door opened, revealing a tall woman of about fifty with untidy grey hair. She wore a purple shawl over a black gown decorated with squares of coloured silk.

"I'm sure you can sing better than that," she said curtly.

Behind her hung a large crucifix. Molly gasped in horror.

"Please," asked Heather. "We're lost. Can you help us?"

"You'd better come in," said the woman.

An altar bearing a pair of candlesticks stood in the spacious hall. Here and there were large statues in flowing robes and sombre pictures of people with strange expressions, except for one of a beautiful lady who had a kindly smile.

"I rescue furnishing from condemned churches. I'm expecting some more tonight. This way."

She led the children into a dimly lit sitting room with a fire crackling in the grate.

"I had better phone your parents."

Heather produced a note from a pocket inside her coat.

"Our number. We've just moved."

The woman lifted the receiver of an old fashioned telephone, pulled around a funny wheel, and let it go, several times.

"Mrs Ingham? Miss Cameron here, Haddon Hall. I have your children with me. They're lost. Would you come and get them?"

The Inghams eventually arrived; their frostiness was almost palpable. They glared at their children.

The knocker hammered again, and Miss Cameron showed in some men who were delivering several large boxes.

"Put them down here, please," she said. "By the fire,"

Having shown the men out, Miss Cameron returned with hot chocolate and mince pies.

"Merry Christmas, my new neighbours. I hope we can get to know each other better. Shall we unpack?"

Gradually, some nativity figures were brought to light.

"They feel cold," said Timmy.

Miss Cameron replenished the logs on the fire. The light from the flickering flames made The Holy Family seem almost alive. Then, tenderly, she began singing

'Silent Night.' The children looked at each other and falteringly joined in. Little by little, their parents slowly began to follow. Timmy nudged his sisters.

"Look," he whispered. "Mum and Dad are holding hands."

Comedy

A NIGHT OUT

Mr Gilmore came into the kitchen, suitably tired and ready for a break.

"Well, dear," he said to his wife, "I've pruned the roses, planted the potatoes, and prepared the ground for my new strawberry plants. I think I'll go up for a nice bath, then come down and enjoy my tea."

He felt he deserved it and was looking forward to a relaxing evening.

"You'll have to make it yourself," said Mrs Gilmore." I'm going out."

He wasn't ready for this. Where was she going?

"I'm meeting Betty in the Museum at five o'clock, and I don't want to be late. One of our knitting circle is giving a talk on local archaeology to raise funds for the hospice. I told you last night. You surely haven't forgotten? We've all promised to support her. I believe they are building a new wing."

"But how long will you be, dear?"

"I'm not sure; a couple of hours maybe. There's a ready meal in the fridge. You just have to pop it in the microwave."

So saying, she put on her hat and coat and left him to his own devices.

"A couple of hours! Archaeology!" Mr Gilmore grumbled to himself. "I don't know why they don't stick to their knitting. At least I might get a jumper out of it."

What did she think she was doing? Well, he knew what she thought she was doing, but the question was; what was he to do about it?

That evening, Mr Gilmore sat down sulkily in his favourite armchair in front of the television. He had finished his ready meal; it wasn't much to write home about, and he was searching the listings for a suitable show.

"Hundreds of channels," he said to himself, "and I can't find anything I like."

He eventually settled upon a local news program and sipped a stiff scotch.

"There's been another robbery at the Higham Museum," said the presenter. "Two more manikins, used for displaying women's historical costumes, have been lifted."

This did not overly perturb Mr Gilmore, and it wasn't long before the scotch had its effect.

He was woken by the telephone. It was Harold, a workmate who lived a couple of roads away. It seemed his wife had gone to the meeting as well.

"Alan, I'm just phoning to see if Millie has arrived home."

"Oh, don't worry, Harold. They're probably just getting down to brass tacks by now."

"But it's eleven o'clock. Surely they should be home by now?"

Good heavens, was that the time?

"Millie, Millie," called Alan. "Are you there?"

But his wife wasn't home either; this was more than a couple of hours. He began to get seriously worried. Anything could have happened.

"Stay there. I'm coming round right away. I'm bringing the camper. Who knows what problems we're going to face."

"Oh, Alan, thank God you've come," said Harold opening the door. "I'm getting really concerned. This isn't like Betty at all, you know. Did Millie say anything to you?"

"Not much, Harold. Only that she was going to the Museum for a talk on local archaeology."

"Perhaps we ought to call the police?"

"Not just yet. We'll try their mobiles first. Has Betty got hers?"

"Of course, Alan. I'm surprised she hasn't called."

"Millie hasn't either. I wonder what's going on."

They both tried phoning their wives, and Harold got a reply, but the reception was terrible.

"Millie - - - me - - - can't - - -," crackled the voice in a harsh staccato.

"She keeps breaking up, Alan. I've no idea what she's saying, but it sounds like they're in trouble."

"This is worrying, Harold. Let's have a scout around before we contact the police. Come on."

At that, they both took off in the camper.

They called at the Museum first, but that was all barred and bolted. They called several members of the knitting circle, but none of them had any idea where they were either. The rest had arrived home safely, around half-past eight and certainly no later than nine.

"Where does this knitting circle meet, Harold? "

"The scout hut, I think."

"It's worth a try."

But that was all in darkness too.

"I don't like it, Alan. We can't delay any longer. We must call the police."

"Hello, Higham Constabulary, PC Stringer here."

The two men told him their problem with great urgency.

"Now, don't worry, gentlemen. I'm sure your wives will be back very soon. I'll just take a few details."

So they answered the officer's questions, getting more and more agitated by the minute.

"Now, there's no need to worry, gentlemen. I have logged the case and will keep an eye out for any developments. There's usually a simple explanation. A signal breaking up like that could mean anything. They may have gone out for the night. I suggest you go home to be ready for their return."

"You're not implying they could have gone clubbing without calling us, are you? The very idea!"

"I'm not implying anything, Mr Gilmore."

"Aren't you going out to look for them? There have been two female manikins nicked from the Museum. What if the thieves have progressed to abduction?"

"I rather doubt it, Mr Gilmore. We are keeping a close eye on those thieves, and if, by chance, your wives are involved with them, we will contact you."

Unable to make any further headway with the police, they both went back to Harold's house, but unfortunately, in his hurry, he had locked himself out.

"That is not very helpful, Harold. You had better come back to my house."

Alan backed the camper into his drive, and the two men got out. Mr Gilmore put his hand in his pocket; then he put his other hand into his other pocket; next, he felt his coat pockets.

"Oh dear, I think I've left my key indoors. There's only one thing to do, and that is to stay in the camper."

Soon they had the light on and were heating some beans on the gas stove, trying to make themselves as comfortable as possible.

"It's a good thing you've got the camper, Alan."

"It would be better if we hadn't locked ourselves out, Harold. Millie's a good wife, you know. She looks after me wonderfully well. Never complains, even though I do tend to be a bit grumpy at times."

"Betty's the same. Always busy. No fuss. I wish I hadn't complained to her about the shopping. We could break in."

"I'm not breaking into my own house, Harold," said Alan. "Millie's sure to be home soon, and she will have a key. Do you think we should break into yours?"

"No, I'm sure you're right, Alan."

Alan poured some stale orange juice into a cup for himself, and Harold finished the bottle.

"We are best just sitting it out, Alan. Your camper is very cosy. All mod cons, eh? Perhaps I could just use the loo?"

"Certainly not. There's no water in the system. You'll have to do the best you can in the garden but mind my begonias."

While Harold was outside, Alan pulled a couple of blankets out from under the seats. It was a cold night, so they would need them. He had forgotten to explain exactly where the begonias were and hoped Harold had gone in the other direction. Suddenly there was a cry of pain from out in the darkness, and eventually, Harold appeared looking more than a little distressed.

"You didn't tell me about the roses, Alan. Oo! They've got sharp thorns."

"Oh no, my roses! I hope you haven't damaged any of my prize blooms."

Alan apologised, and said he didn't think he had, then reclined rather gingerly opposite Alan.

At about six o'clock in the morning, Harold was woken by loud tapping and pattering on the roof.

"Alan, Alan. Are you awake?"

"I am now," said Alan sleepily. "What is it?"

"There's a strange noise outside."

They both lay awake in the half-light listening.

"There it is again," whispered Harold. "You don't think…."

"No, I don't. It's only birds," said Alan, fully awake. "They live in the tree next door. I do wish they wouldn't use my camper roof as a dance floor. We won't get any sleep now they've started."

Harold got up.

"Where are you going, Harold?"

"To shoo them away."

"Leave them. They'll only come back again. We've had no word from the police, have we?"

Indeed they hadn't. Then the realisation dawned on Alan that he had given the police his home phone number and, as he had locked himself out, was in no position to hear it let alone answer.

"Alan, I think we ought to call the police and give them your mobile number."

"Why mine?

"Because mine needs charging. The battery has just run out."

"Oh, for goodness sake. Very well."

Upon hearing the women hadn't returned home, the constable on duty assured them that they would begin enquiries the very next day.

"There's nothing else for it, Harold. We'll have to continue the search ourselves. You can charge your phone from the cigarette lighter. Here's the connector. Now, let's go. I suggest we call in at the nearest hotel to make ourselves comfortable and get some breakfast. At least the police have my mobile number now."

The two friends were tucking into a full English breakfast when Alan received a call.

"It's Marjorie from the knitting circle. Has Millie come home yet?"

"No, she hasn't. Neither has Betty."

"Oh, dear. Perhaps we should go back to the Museum to see what's going on there. I'll meet you by the dinosaurs."

"Good idea," said Alan. "We're on our way. We'll see you there." Alan drained his cup of coffee. "Come on, Harold. We're meeting Marjorie at the Museum."

Harold wrapped his remaining slice of toast in a napkin, put it in his pocket, and they both made for the exit.

They found Marjorie with the Assistant Curator, who had a key that a cleaner had handed in that morning.

"I think I know where it's from," he said. "Follow me."

The meeting room was not exceptionally large. It had a parquet floor, oak panelling, and smelled strongly of furniture polish. There was a substantial table under the window and half a dozen chairs lined up against the opposite wall.

"It doesn't look like they had a very big meeting," Harold commented. How old is this building?"

"It was originally the home of the O'Leary family in the 17th century. When all of the family had died, it became an inn of rather ill repute, I believe. Then in the nineteenth century, it was an asylum for the criminally insane. It housed several infamous locals such as Jack the Nipper and Tweeny Sod. There are tales of it being haunted or something. Only this morning, a young man we had recently engaged as a night watchman came back in a frightful state, saying he had heard all sorts of strange noises, bangings, and moans. He refused to work here a moment longer and gave in his notice there and then."

At that point, muffled cries came as if from thin air. A shiver went down Harold's spine.

"I don't think the girls are here, Alan. Let's go."

"Get a grip of yourself, Harold. There's nothing to be afraid of."

The cries came again, and Alan's face drained of colour.

The Assistant Curator thrust the key in one of the panels, twisted it with some difficulty, and began to push the door open.

"Well, who would have thought it!" exclaimed Alan.

The door, however, had only opened a few inches when women's voices came from within.

"Oh, thank God you've come. We thought we would be here forever."

"Millie, Betty," called Alan and Harold. "Don't worry; we'll have you out."

The door seemed jammed, but the Assistant Curator managed to get his hand inside.

"There's a chair jamming the door. I think I can move it."

"Don't, don't," shouted Betty. "Or the whole stack of chairs will come down on us."

"It Looks like we'll have to take the panel off," he conceded and went to find the joiner.

The screws were very rusty, and most of the heads broke off.

The joiner carefully eased a screwdriver under the panel and gave it a sharp wrench. All of a sudden, there was a loud rending sound as the old screws gave way.

"Look out," shouted Alan.

And the panel fell to the floor under an avalanche of chairs.

"What happened?" asked Alan

"Well," Millie began, "we volunteered to put the chairs away while the others went home. We had got most of them stacked when a draught blew the door closed with us inside."

"And we had left the key outside," Betty added. "We tried to open the door, but it wouldn't budge, would it, Millie?"

"No. There must be something odd about the catch. It was pitch black. A chair fell from one of the stacks and just missed us. We were afraid the others might collapse any minute, so we kept well away at the back of the passage."

"What happened to your mobiles?" Harold interrupted.

"We couldn't get them to work," said Millie.

The Assistant Curator explained, "I'm afraid the oak cladding, the stone brickwork, and the thick ivy outside makes any signal very difficult."

"Why didn't you shout for help?" said Alan.

"We did. Betty and I were crying out and banging on the walls all night, but it seemed no one could hear us. We had almost given up hope until we heard your voices faintly through the wall."

"We were so relieved to hear you both," said Betty. "Now, all we need is to go home for a cup of tea and a good breakfast."

"There's just one problem, Betty. Alan and I have locked ourselves out. We've been out all night. "

"Oh, a fine pair you are! It's a good thing I've got my key. What about you, Millie?"

Millie fished in her handbag. "Yes, here's mine. Let's get them home."

At that point, PC Stringer made an appearance.

"Well, Sir," he said to the Assistant Curator. "We've solved the problem of the manikins. We found your night watchman in Higham woods in a terrible state. It seems he's been involved in dealing with drugs, which were concealed in the manikins. He came out with some story about the Museum being haunted and refused to return there ever again."

"It's a fine thing you coming in right now," Alan complained. "You've more interest in a pair of manikins than rescuing our wives. They're the ghosts that frightened your drug runner."

They made their way out of the room, quickening their pace, as a chilly draught and a long mournful sigh issued from the open panel.

DORIS'S LITTLE BREAK

"Derek, I'm just calling to see if Sammy is alright. Yes, I know I'm getting a bit overanxious, but he's never been away before. Oh, is he? That's good. Can you put the phone to him so I can hear him purr?"

There was a pause while Doris Harrison's son tried to catch the cat, but the claws were out, and it certainly wasn't inclined to purr. So Derek was obliged to do his best at an imitation of a cat purr.

"There you are, Mum, he's fine. A home from home."

"Thank you, dear. And don't forget to give him his piece of steamed fish before he goes to bed at night."

"No, Mum, I won't forget. Now don't worry. He'll be fine. And I'll keep an eye on the house as well. Just make sure you have a good time."

"Thank you, dear. I don't know what I'd do without you."

Doris Harrison put the phone down and looked in her handbag for the umpteenth time. The tickets, her passport, yes, everything was there.

Suddenly, a car horn made her jump. She looked out of the window. A taxi had pulled up with her friend Edna inside. Doris put her modest pull-along case on the front doorstep, set the burglar alarm, and locked the door of her little terrace house, her refuge in Collier Street, before whispering a fond goodbye and making her way to the waiting car.

"Would you wait a minute, please?" she asked the driver. "I must leave this with Mrs Fothergill."

166

She dropped a key through her neighbour's letterbox and then all of a sudden began to wish she hadn't agreed to go away. It was all so exciting at the time. At this moment, however, she wished she could change her mind. Was everything switched off and locked up? She'd used the iron that morning. Yes, yes, she was sure it was off. There was no turning back now. Besides, her friend would never forgive her. She was always the strong one, even at school.

"What took you, Doris?"

"Oh, nothing, Edna."

"A funny sort of nothing that was. Now come on. We're going to enjoy ourselves."

"The airport, please," they both said in unison.

Then sat back, giggling nervously, and chattering excitedly like pair of school girls.

Doris had been widowed for over ten tears, and it was a lot longer since she'd had anything that could be called a decent break. Her son and granddaughter had often pressed her to take a little holiday, but without success until now.

"Granny, it would do you good to get away for a while. There are so many lovely places that you would enjoy seeing. And there's no reason now why you shouldn't."

Coming out from a Townswomen's Guild meeting one afternoon, having heard a most enjoyable talk entitled Travelling Light, the two pensioners had decided to take the plunge together and go on a short vacation. Nothing fancy, just a bit of a breather. They arranged to meet the following week at Up and Away, the travel agent in their local shopping centre.

"We'll see what they have to say," said Edna; "then we can mull it all over while we have tea and scones in Aggie's Caf'."

Within the week, to the complete surprise, at least, of Doris's family, the two friends had booked a week's holiday abroad.

"I've never done anything like this before," said Doris. "I will need a lot of help and advice. And I'm very nervous about flying. It's my first time, you know."

"I've flown before," said Edna. "There's no need to worry. Nothing to it."

"But that was nearly fifty years ago," said Doris. "And then it was only to Prestwick."

"Yes, well. I don't suppose it's a lot different now. Just follow me and do what I do."

"Derek was very concerned to know where we were going, but I wouldn't tell him. It's our secret."

"Quite right too, Doris. What business is it of his anyway?"

"I suppose I should have done Edna. He does worry about me but having a little secret like this is so exciting. I think I reassured him a bit, though, by promising to send him a postcard."

Under the guidance of the travel representative, feverish preparations had been made. There were passports and visas to apply for, foreign money to be exchanged, to say nothing of shopping for clothes and other personal belongings.

"Doris," said Edna after storming Marks and Spencer's. "You'll never be able to get all that in your little suitcase."

"I just want to have an alternative, Edna. In case I change my mind at the last moment."

The night before their flight, neither of them got much sleep; they were still rearranging their cases; putting in this, taking out that; always with an eye on the alarm clock; terrified of sleeping in.

The taxi finally pulled up at terminal one.

"Here we are, girls," said the driver. "Have a good trip and behave yourselves."

More laughter.

The vastness of the airport building, the crowds, other travellers, and noise began to wither Doris's enthusiasm.

"What's the matter, Doris? It's only like the market on a Saturday morning. Let's ask this man here in the uniform. I'm sure he'll help us."

Once they were on the plane, they tried to relax.

"This is better," said Doris. "I didn't like that young man who checked our cases."

"No," said Edna. "Fancy taking our thermos flasks off us. Said we couldn't take them on the plane."

"I thought he was very mean."

"Said it was because of security. What did he think we were going to do with them, for goodness sake? I'm going to write a strongly worded letter of complaint to the airport authorities when we get back."

"Good for you, Ed. I might write one myself."

Doris stood up and began searching in the locker above her.

"What's up, Dot?"

"I'm looking for our parachutes, Ed."

"I don't think there are any."

Suddenly, in a panic, Doris grabbed hold of her friend's arm.

"Oh, Ed, what are we going to do?"

Edna shook her off.

"Control yourself, Doris. You heard what was said about the emergency procedures the same as me. Don't worry. We'll be down soon enough."

This did nothing to allay Doris's fears, so Edna decided they should have a drink and tried to attract a flight attendant's attention.

A woman in uniform eventually arrived with a trolley and asked if there was anything they would like.

"We'd like our flasks back," demanded Edna grimly.

The flight attendant began to explain why it was not possible, but Edna cut her short.

"Spare us the gory details. We'll have a couple of cocoas instead."

Still, in quite a state of agitation, Doris made her request.

"Could I have a parachute, please?"

"Of course," said the attendant. "Would you like it with pumpkin or Pernod?"

Completely bewildered by this, Doris's reply was quite incoherent.

As usual, Edna took control.

"Take no notice of her. It's her first flight. We'll just have the cocoa if you don't mind."

But it seemed even cocoa was off the menu, so they settled for hot chocolate.

After a long flight, they arrived safely and began to enjoy life at their hotel. The next day they were taken on a whirlwind tour of the city and returned with their heads spinning after seeing ultra-modern buildings, glittering entertainment palaces, and familiar landmarks they were convinced should have been elsewhere in the world.

With still an hour before their evening meal, they relaxed beside the swimming pool sipping Pina Coladas that Edna had purchased at the bar. Doris looked at hers, resplendent with its plastic monkey and paper sunshade.

"What did you say these were called, Ed?"

Edna looked a bit vague. They'd had such a busy day.

"I'm not sure. I think the barman said they were called Pink Colanders or something. Anyway, he put everything into what looked a bit like a Thermos flask and then started shaking it up. In fact, he did quite a juggling act."

Doris found this rather puzzling. How could a drink be made in a colander? Surely it would come out of the holes. She giggled.

"it's very nice anyway. I think I'm feeling a bit squiffy."

Edna took a postcard from her handbag and began writing a message.

"Oh, that's a good idea, Ed. I think I'll do mine as well. I couldn't make my mind up which card to have."

"I know. I thought I'd never get you out of that shop."

"I got one with the pyramid on. What about yours?"

Edna held up the card she was writing, showing a large sphinx.

"People will wonder where we are," she declared.

"The only problem is," said Doris, "I haven't seen any post boxes yet."

Edna took a sip of her drink.

"There are a couple outside the hotel, Dot. Those blue things. They're called mailboxes out here.

"I had no idea. I thought they were rubbish bins. I put a banana skin in one."

Edna gave her a withering look.

"Really, Doris" We can't take you anywhere."

"Well, how was I to know?" she said feebly.

"It does say LETTERS on the side, Doris. Didn't you notice?"

"Oh, dear! I thought it said LITTER."

Rather tentatively, Doris began to write her card, but Edna took it from her.

"Here, let me do it for you. You won't be able to write straight after that drink. Now, what do you want to say?"

"I don't know, Ed. What do you suggest?"

"Why not begin, wish you were here, like everyone else.

"I can't just say that, Ed."

It seemed a good enough start.

"Who is it for, Dot?"

"My Derek."

"Well, why not say something about the weather and what you've been doing?"

"Dear Derek." Doris began. "Wish you were here. The weather is hot and sunny. There is plenty to see and do. Lots of entertainment, and I've even met a young man that looks just like Elvis Presley. Oh, he is lovely."

"Steady on, Doris."

"I have won hundreds of dollars but, unfortunately, lost most of it. Edna and I are both having a wonderful time here in – Where are we, Ed?"

"Las Vegas."

"Oh yes. Love, Mum."

OUR HOLIDAY

"Are we nearly there yet?" came a little voice from the back seat.

"Not far now, Harry," said Dad.

This had been going on ever since we left home, but now there really seemed a good chance we were actually getting somewhere.

"Everyone, look for a wigwam," shouted Dad as we sped past endless fields and farmyards.

We knew what he meant. This was the sign for a campsite, and in particular, hopefully, our holiday destination. We were all looking forward to spending a whole week in our new tent. Well, it wasn't really new; Dad had bought it for a song two months before on the internet. However, having compartments as well as an awning, it was almost as exciting as a new house.

My little brother Harry and I, with our older sister Jenny, had enjoyed trying it out in the back garden, eating bacon butties. Once, we spent the whole night in it; Harry and I did anyway; you know what sisters are like. Jenny tried to take over as Mother, but we weren't having any of it; we didn't want to be put to bed; we wanted to stay up and tell ghost stories, so she went back into the house saying she was scared. Scared? I don't think so!

We set out early on a grey August morning; Mum map reading in case the satnav led us up some un-navigable route. We had been travelling all day when

Mum said, "Liam, I'm sure we should have turned off two miles back."

"Trust me, Mandy, I know what I'm doing," said Dad. "We have the latest satnav equipment."

So, we continued on and on until we came to what looked like a camping sign, which we followed down a narrow track. By now, the night was drawing on, and even with our strong headlights, the darkness seemed to close in from every side. Finally, Dad pulled up short as, all at once, we came upon a signpost with an arrow pointing to the left.

"This is it", he said.

"Are you sure?" said Mum. "It doesn't look very inviting."

"This is real camping, Mandy. You'll love it in the morning."

So saying, he got out and, with some difficulty, opened an old iron farm gate, went to a hut just inside the field, and knocked on the door.

"They must have shut for the night. I'll call on the camp manager in the morning."

"It's a bit muddy, Liam," said Mum as we turned into the gateway.

That was an understatement.

"Just as well we've got the four-by-four", Dad said confidently. "We'll pitch camp further up the hill, so it shouldn't be so bad."

He was right; it wasn't, the only problem was the car got stuck. Cursing, Dad unhitched the trailer.

"Mandy, Vince, Jenny, give me a push."

So, after a great deal of revving, the vehicle lurched forward while we, covered in mud, staggered up the hill with the trailer.

The sky leaked continually while we set up camp.

First, Dad unpacked the tent from its trailer and began to arrange the poles.

"Come on, give me a hand. Here Vince, help me put these together. Jenny, you hold that pole, and Harry, this one. We'll soon have it up. Mandy, did you bring the instructions?"

"I thought you had them."

"Then they must still be on the sideboard."

"They weren't there when we left."

Tired, cold and wet, we were missing our warm house. Harry's tearful complaints soon increased to a full-throated wail.

"I want to go home!"

So Mum took him back to the car to comfort him.

By about one a.m., we had covered the frame and put the groundsheet down.

"Can I let go now?" came a small voice in a dark corner. No one had noticed Harry's return, but there he was, holding up one of the poles.

"It's OK, Harry. You can let go now. We'll be in bed soon."

So Harry let go of the pole. It fell with a *boing* onto the groundsheet; the tent looked like it was about to follow as Mum entered with the bedding. I thought Dad would explode; then Harry pulled something out of his knapsack.

"I've got the picture," he said, quite unaware he had the assembly instructions.

Dad didn't know whether to laugh or cry. So instead, he went outside and gave a loud, agonised yell.

"Liam, dear, you'll wake the other campers," said Mum gently.

It was nearly three a.m. when we finally crawled into our sleeping bags. Canned beans and sausages had never tasted so good, while the warmth from the camp stove and the gas lantern prepared us for sleep. Thankfully the rain had stopped, and a full moon had risen above the treetops, its silvery beams softly illuminating the canvas. So all was peaceful until strange shadows were seen of things moving about outside, accompanied by muffled rustlings and trampling.

"What's that?" whispered Harry.

"I don't know," I said, beginning to feel a bit fearful myself.

"It's the zombies coming to get us," said Jenny.
Just then, there was a sound from outside like a deep, strangled cough. Well, that did it. Harry let out a terrified squeal and insisted on snuggling down with Mum and Dad in their sleeping bag. I lay petrified in my cocoon while Jenny tried to contain her giggles. Nobody got any sleep that night.

We must have slept to some extent, though, because we woke to bright sunshine streaming in through the plastic windows and the sound of Dad shaving while whistling the theme to 'The Great Escape'.

"It's very quiet. Aren't the neighbours up yet?" he asked as Mum came in from the car with the breakfast cereal.

"Oh, they're up alright. Go on; shoo, shoo," she said, trying to drive back a group of large bovine faces looking curiously through the tent entrance. "There are your zombies."

"Can we get some milk from them?" said Harry.

"No, Harry," said Mum emphatically. "I think we should stick to what we've got in the cold box."

After breakfast, Dad went out to have a good look at our surroundings.

"I'm sorry, folks. It appears we've come to the wrong place,"

We could have told him that.

"The shed is an animal feed store or something."

"But what about the sign at the gate?" asked Mum.

"Oh, that's just to show ramblers; this is supposed to be a public footpath; it's got a little footprint on it. He keyed in a number on his mobile phone, and we all waited for the reply.

After a short but rather tense conversation, Dad said he knew now where the site was and that we would soon be there. The receptionist had told him we could reach it if we continued along the road we were on. Later, we discovered we could have got there a lot quicker if Dad had turned at the junction two miles back as Mum told him, but all she said was, "Anyone can make a mistake, dear. You did well to get us almost there without any setback."

178

We packed up the tent and equipment, Dad making sure the assembly instructions were safe, then he hitched up the trailer, and we began to head for the gate. But, unfortunately, Dad hadn't closed it properly the night before, and to our horror, the cows had strayed out of it.

"Don't worry," he said. "I'll soon get them in."

He opened the gate wide and followed them down the lane, intending to drive them back. Mum, however, got out of the car, shaking the cereal packet and shouting, "I think this may help, dear."

Suddenly, the cows became very animated and eager to return to the field.

"No, Mandy, no!" yelled Dad as they pursued him back up the track.

He just about managed to reach the gate in time to vault over it as they all charged through. I had never seen him move so fast. It was like an old western movie.

"Quickly, dear, close the gate," said Mum keeping the cows occupied with the cornflakes.

"What do you think you're doing on my land," said a stern-looking man in a cloth cap and waxed jacket. "This is private property. Can't you read the sign on the gate?"

We hadn't seen that one, and he was not amused.

"I could have lost all my cows if an aeroplane had gone over, as they sometimes do. The R.A.F base isn't far away, you know."

Dad apologised profusely, explained the mistake we had made, and offered to pay for staying the night in his field.

"You keep your money, sir. You'll need it; it's expensive enough where you're going but watch where you set up camp next time."

Dad thanked him and, feeling suitably chastened, pulled out of the gate, back to the main road.

We eventually reached 'The Zoro Adventure Park and Camp Site.' The rest of the week passed without incident, well, almost. Harry got lost at one point. Mum was frantic, and everyone joined in the search. We finally found him feeding the rabbits in the children's zoo.

"Can I have one?" he said.

"Well, we'll have to see," said Mum.

This usually meant no. He didn't give up asking, though, and soon after we got home, Zoro the rabbit joined the family.

Faith & Life

TEARS OF WETHERWELL

A small group of people gathered at the Parish Church of Wetherwell to watch a long bundle being raised from the clay of a newly dug grave. It was an ancient oak statue of The Madonna that a gravedigger had come across in the course of his duties. Its wrapping of cloth and bark had all but disintegrated though they appeared to have protected it from the worst ravages of time, and after an initial clean-up, she still bore a regal countenance in her flowing robes and Saxon crown.

"A rare find," said one man."

"It could well have been hidden there for safekeeping at the time of the Reformation," said another.

The carving was in surprisingly good condition. The Infant Christ, cradled in one arm, was easily identifiable, but what she held in her other hand had badly deteriorated.

"A lily perhaps, or even a mace," said a man in a blue anorak.

"She has a beautiful face," said a woman taking photographs. "It's one of the best examples of medieval carving I've seen. We must make every effort to save it."

Having come to light now, there was no time to lose in preserving it. So the statue was taken to a museum in York, where it could be treated using the latest techniques. First, a percussion of cameras captured in detail the original appearance of the carving, then again later, after the procedures had been carried out.

"Steady now," said one of the archaeologists as it was packed away. "It's very delicate."

Shortly after these events, the funeral of Albert Dewhurst took place. He was sorely missed, not only by his family but by a large proportion of the community, and the creation of a suitable memorial was mooted. Parish records showed that a statue originally occupied a niche at the church doorway, but it had disappeared during a riot in the late nineteenth century. Eventually, a proposal was passed to have one made in Albert's memory and site it in the vacant cavity. All agreed that a copy of the figure so recently discovered would be most fitting and that funds from a current Lottery grant should be made available for this purpose.

"We have our very own craftsman here in the village," said Father McNally.

He was a diminutive priest whose good intentions did not always bear fruit in the way that he might wish.

"I'm sure he would be the ideal person to do it. Unfortunately, he doesn't attend church anymore since his wife died, hit by a car, a terrible tragedy,"

There were murmurs of sympathy.

"I believe she was pregnant," said a woman on the committee. "He must be heartbroken."

Another member said, "Do you think you could have a quiet word with him, Father?"

"Of course; the first chance I get,"

Lewis Phinn was a thick-set man in his thirties. His large dextrous hands, used to shaping stone and wood, caressed a chunk of limestone standing about four feet

183

high, which had recently been delivered to his workshop from the Sherburn quarry. He had seen a face in the irregularities of that particular piece of rock, a fleeting glimpse, but he'd definitely seen it, so there was no doubt that this had to be the piece to use for the statue. The face had been beautiful, compassionate, and loving, but there seemed no way he could recapture it again except in his memory. Try as he might, he could only manage to sketch a poor resemblance. He had, of course, a much clearer memory of his wife, so it wasn't her. His child should have been born about now, and he felt somewhat unsettled about taking on this commission.

Father McNally had accosted him a few weeks before in the street.

"Ah, Lewis. Just the man. We were wondering if you would be prepared to make a statue to fit the empty niche outside the church doorway."

He explained what had happened and the decision the committee had come to. After some thought, Lewis had grudgingly acceded to their request, though deep down, he was flattered. So what if he didn't go to church?

Trawling the museum's website, through pages of archaeological theory and speculation about the statue's discovery, Lewis eventually came to the photographs. Astounded by what he saw, he looked away in disbelief. No, it wasn't possible. Slowly he turned to look again at the pictures, indeed one particular close-up. There it was, that face, the face of the figure. It bore a strong resemblance to the one he'd seen at Sherburn.

Lewis watched his design turn through various projections on his computer screen. Yes, it needed changing here a little and a bit more there, but it was enough to provide a reasonable working model. With some trepidation, he took a mallet to a large chisel and made the initial cut to release the figure from the stone. The work was slow and painstaking, but he became totally absorbed in it. For many days he continued chipping away pieces of stone that weren't part of the end product. Hours went by daily when mugs of coffee were left almost undrunk on his workbench as he continued to refine his handiwork from one angle and another. He was never completely satisfied with any of his work; there was always some fault that only he would notice, but it would urge him on to chip away and smooth out minor projections and convexities until there was nothing further he could do to improve it.

Father McNally conducted a simple dedication ceremony attended by members of the Dewhurst family and other people of the community as the statue was mortared into its damp niche. It attracted the villagers' interest for a good many weeks, but eventually, this waned as the figure began to blend in with the patina of the surrounding stonework.

A year or so later, a child and her mother were waiting at a bus stop outside the church. After a hard winter, the spring sun warmed the frozen stones. From a crack at the base of the Madonna, a tiny blue flower had pushed its way up and bloomed.

"Look at the pretty flower Mummy. Can I pick it?"

"No, dear, it belongs to the Lady."

At that moment, a man came to clean the walls outside of the church. He scrubbed the stones with a stiff brush skimming over the statue to remove any loose bits of detritus. He then swept up the dirt, pulled the flower from its crack, and took it all around the back of the building. The little girl looked on horrified.

"Mummy, that man has just taken the Lady's flower."

"I know, dear. What a shame."

After nearly half an hour, the bus finally came, and the little girl glanced back at the figure in its niche.

"Look, Mummy, the Lady's crying."

Several others, waiting to board, turned to look also, and certainly, there was water dripping from the statue's eyes.

Lewis put his tools down abruptly, his concentration shattered. A lad who helped him occasionally had burst into his workshop.

"Jimmy, how often have I told you not to...?"

"Sorry, Mr Phinn, but there's a TV film crew outside. They want to talk with you about your crying statue."

"Two things wrong, Jimmy; that's not my statue; I only made it. Secondly, it does not cry."

"Oh, but it does, Mr Phinn. All the people in the village have seen it."

"I haven't seen it cry. Have you?"

"I'm not sure, Mr Phinn. Only when the rain's in the right direction."

"There you are then. They're just credulous devotees. They'll believe in anything. You know very well it's just a lump of rock. You were there when I began carving it."

"They won't go away, Mr Phinn."

"Then it will be a very short program," said Lewis moodily. What was he going to say to them about some gullible and impressionable so-called pilgrims?

Sizeable crowds were beginning to gather daily outside the church around the statue, chanting prayers, singing hymns, laying flowers, and cramming petitions into the niche. Candles had been burning, but the rain and wind had put them out. A man pointed at Lewis.

"There he is. The one who made the statue."

Several people tripped across the road to talk with him.

"Oh, you are greatly blessed," said one.

"Very talented," said another.

A woman grabbed his hand and kissed it.

"The finger of God!" she said,

"Leave me alone," protested Lewis. "I'm just an ordinary craftsman. I don't even believe in God."

"Oh, how humble," said several of the pilgrims amongst each other.

"Give me your blessing," said one.

Lewis tapped him on the head to rid himself of the attention, but then they all wanted blessing.

"That's enough. I have work to do," said Lewis walking briskly down the street followed by a train of ardent disciples.

The windows of private houses were filled with religious artefacts, obviously for sale, and Father McNally recognised several from Mrs Hesketh's parlour now put on display in her window. There were even statues that looked similar to the one in the niche, but none quite the same. Reproductions of Wetherwell's very own Madonna would be very sought after, and Lewis could clean up.

He downsized the plans on his computer and quickly began roughing one out from a length of pine. It was rather coarse, but with a little extra attention, it might be acceptable. He made a few more and soon had half a dozen in various stages of completion. He cut off their superfluous edges, sanded and polished the little figures, then sold them to a neighbour who had turned his home into a gift shop and promoted them as, *Made by the creator of the Weeping Madonna of Wetherwell.* Within a week, they were devoured at ten times the price.

Nightly, a light burned in the workshop window, often well into the small hours. Lewis was beginning to make a substantial profit but had little time for breakfast. The figures were his only thought. One morning after another late night, he wondered if he could afford a copying machine. It would make life easier, and he would be able to turn out a greater quantity of statues. He was cutting out another one when suddenly a searing pain seized his hand as the bandsaw bit into it. Immediately he switched off the machine while blood began to flood the bench. He grabbed some rag to try and stem the flow and called a cab.

"Hello, a taxi immediately, for the Friarage Hospital."

"No cabs available at the moment."

"There must be one. It's an emergency."

"Be about an hour. They're all busy with pilgrims."

At the church, he tried to flag one down, waving his bloody hand.

One taxi passed by, occupied, then another just the same.

"Pick thee up in a jif' mate," shouted a driver from an empty car as he sailed away. Would he?

One of Lewis's clients who served at a makeshift piety stall owed him a favour, but would he be able to leave it? Where were his friends when he needed them? Did he have any? Father McNally came out of the church, beaming.

"Father, I need to get to the Friarage."

"I'll see to you after, Lewis. I'm just about to take a service. Oh, there's Deacon Graham; ask him. I'm sure he'll help you."

Father McNally scurried back inside. No doubt he'd give an encouraging sermon then send the plate round. Deacon Graham, however, was besieged by people asking him to sign cards, bless candles and take petitions. Obviously, Lewis was not on his radar. The voices of pilgrims in animated conversation became a bewildering cacophony as the crowd pushed past towards the church doorway. Then a soft voice stood out.

"Is there anything I can do?"

He turned and saw a woman about the same age as himself, with dark wavy hair. The lines in her face betrayed stress in her life that may still be ongoing.

"You're hurt. Could I take you somewhere?"

"I really need to get to the Friarage hospital in North Allerton. There's a good Urgent Treatment centre there."

"My car is a fair walk away. It's so busy here. Friends call me Mel. Short for Imelda."

"Thanks, I'm very grateful. My name's Lewis. Lewis Phinn."

Scent from the deodoriser swaying gently from the rear-view mirror had a calming effect on him.

"I'd drive myself, but as you can see..." he lifted his hand.

"It looks painful. What happened?"

"An argument with a bandsaw. Straight on here and turn right at the next junction."

"How far is this medical centre?"

"About 20 miles from the village. It was lucky you came along."

"I don't believe in luck. Things happen for a reason. My son is about to have an operation for a heart condition. I've come to light a candle for him."

"That's tough. And I was bothered about a scratch on my hand."

"Judging by the blood stains, it's more than a scratch."

They drove on in silence through moorland with dry-stone walls, over green hills flecked with spring lambs.

"How old is he, your son?"

"Five and a half."

"He'll be needing you. I'm sorry to take you out of your way."

"It's OK. His Grandmother is with him."

"Go left at the next junction. It's not far now."

"What makes me think you've been there before?"

"I've had a few cuts and scrapes."

With his hand treated and dressed, Lewis returned with Mel to Wetherwell.

"It's getting late," he said. "I'm sure my Mother would put you up."

"I must get back to my son," said Mel. "He'll be missing me. I live near Harrogate. About thirty miles away."

"Of course. Could you just wait here a minute?"

Lewis hurried to his workshop, struggled with the key, and then returned with one of his figures of the Weeping Madonna.

"Here, take this. It's not much."

"Did you make this?"

"It's only tourist tat, I'm afraid. Very rough and ready."

"It's charming. Thank you."

"It may bring you luck."

"Not luck, Lewis, hope, and that's what I need right now."

"A little bit of bread and no cheese," called a yellowhammer from the top of a gorse bush. Lewis was resting with a packed lunch against a dry stone wall gazing across the dale towards home. Mrs Mawson had phoned him that morning. There was an urgency in her voice.

"I must have some more of your statues A.S.A.P. at least a couple of dozen. I've sold all those I bought from you last week; now, most of my customers are going to *Pilgrim Piety* further down the road."

Lewis drove back to his workshop, then walked down to Mrs Mawson's to assure her he would supply them and, more importantly, to negotiate a higher price.

"How's your hand?"

The voice was familiar, but for a moment, he didn't recognise Mel; her face was so different, all the tension had gone.

"There'll be a scar, but it's a lot better. Thanks for asking. It's good to be able to use it again. How's your son?"

"There are still health checks and consultations to go through, but there's been a lot of improvement. Michael's much more lively now. The operation seems to have been a big success. It's like a miracle."

Miracle, a miracle! A bystander pricked up her ears. Hearsay spread rapidly among the pilgrims.

"Are the statues blessed?" asked a woman in a gift shop.

"These things don't happen in this day and age," said a man to his partner over a bowl of soup.

"Excuse me miss."

A man in slim-fitting jeans, an open-neck shirt, and a khaki jacket stopped Mel as she unlocked her car.

He waved a notebook. "A word with you about the miracle, please."

"I'm sorry, I can't tell you anything."

"Just a few minutes, for the Gazette."

Soon others turned up. Cameras clicking and recording booms thrust at her. All asking questions, jostling and bickering amongst each other.

"My son is recovering from a heart operation. That's all I can say."

Unappeased, they pressed her.

"The miracle? Was he healed?"

"Ask at Leeds General Infirmary."

Mel fought her way into the car and, pushing through the media furore, sped off down the high street. Later, she saw on her television the surgeon that had performed the operation making a statement to the press.

"This was a difficult ground-breaking procedure, so success is very uncertain. We can only do our job as well as humanly possible, but ultimately, full recovery lies with a higher power than ours."

Landladies were now turning away guests.

"I'm sorry, we're fully booked. Try the Tourist Information Centre in Masham Market, but I doubt if you will find anywhere closer than Ripon."

Any precious tears that happened to fall from the statue were immediately treasured in phials, and even on tissues, by devotees, while unscrupulous traders peddled bottles of tap water at inflated prices labelled Tears from the Madonna of Wetherwell, as one pilgrim pointed out -

"She would have to be crying an awful lot to supply all the tears that are being sold."

Mrs Murphy entered Father McNally's study with a large cardboard box overflowing with letters. She was a typical Irish Mammy who didn't tolerate idiots and schemers.

"Here's the post, Father. Mostly petitions, I imagine. The mail's increased tenfold since this talk of miracles started."

"Don't scorn them, Mrs Murphy. Many contain donations, and that means we will be able to start repairs to the church."

"Oh, and Father, there's a letter from the Bishop amongst them as well. If you ask me, this affair started with tears, so it will all end in tears."

Father McNally attended his appointment with the Bishop, apprehensive of the outcome.

"Father, I need to know the truth of the reports I am receiving about the events in your parish. Such hysteria is very troubling."

"Your Grace, my church is filled with faithful souls and those seeking guidance. I can now afford repairs and even improvements without depleting diocesan funds. Surely that is a good thing?"

"Possibly, but the Church is not founded on fanaticism. It is important that the truth behind this phenomenon is thoroughly investigated."

"What does your Grace propose?"

"I shall arrange for the statue to be removed and examined by a team of experts which will include scientists such as geologists, forensic geologists, and geophysicists."

"Oh, but, your Grace, people are coming daily expecting to see it and attend services."

"I realise that, Father, which is why I am allowing you time to give notice through the media such as newspapers, radio and television, as well as the social media, to ensure those wishing to visit are informed well in advance. You will also need to contact those in charge of accommodation by letter and email so that bookings may be rescheduled. I will allow you a month for this. That should be a reasonable period."

"But your Grace... "

"This is of the utmost importance, Father, so I would be obliged if you would assist me."

"Yes, your Grace."

Julia Holmes looked through her list of bookings and sighed. Most of them were cancelled. In the gift shop next door, a couple of tourists came in asking about the Weeping Madonna.

"I'm sorry," said Mrs Jessop. "It had to be taken away for investigation by order of the Bishop."

"My wife will be very disappointed," said the gentleman, brushing a hair from his suit. "She gets headaches, and we were hoping to collect a little of the holy water."

"There is an ancient spring nearby associated with St Alkelda, our local saint. The waters there are said to have healing properties. You may get some help at the Tourist Office in Middleham."

"Father," Mrs Murphy shouted from the front door, "There are some villagers outside wanting to see you. They're very concerned about their trade."

"Tell them I'm busy," Father McNally called from his study. "I can't see anyone now."

"We want the statue back!" Their demands reverberated through the hallway. "Our businesses are suffering!"

The Dog and Partridge was almost empty too, and Lewis sat gazing into his beer, then at the scar on his hand. The statues were no longer wanted, so he'd taken on some restoration work at Harewood House a few miles from Harrogate.

Business was brisk as usual at Illingworth's on the Old Bath Road. Tradesmen were coming, buying the tools and hardware they needed and leaving, while many of the D.I.Y. customers were less sure. Lewis was looking amongst the adhesives for some repairs he was doing to the lavish Robert Adam ceiling in the Gallery of the west wing.

"Fancy seeing you here."

Lewis was pleased to see Mel with her son Michael.

"I'm doing some restoration work in Harewood House," he said.

"Oh, it's a wonderful place," exclaimed Mel. "The history, and the architecture. They're very fortunate to have you."

"I was fortunate to get the job."

"Yes," Mel agreed. "I heard the bubble had burst in the village, but you are good at your job."

"He's looking well," Lewis said, indicating Michael. "Your husband must be relieved."

"Oh him," said Mell scornfully. "He packed his things and left soon after Michael was diagnosed. I haven't seen him since."

Tap, tap, tap - Lewis was chipping out an epitaph one autumn morning when a missile crashed through the window of his workshop. He removed the newspaper wrapping and found the head of the Madonna. The headline ran, FAKE TEARS AT WETHERWELL. A full-page spread in that morning's Gazette reported the results of the tests. The findings endorsed the opinion of the experts that there must be a cavity in the head, finally revealed by X-rays. Water was discovered to have dripped from the ceiling of the niche, settling in the Madonna's crown. It had then filtered through the limestone of the statue and collected in this space. During the winter, the water had frozen and caused a hairline crack across the eyes from which it leaked after the thaw. Lewis examined the head. The fracture was quite obvious now after the abuse it had received.

As he went out to buy a copy of the newspaper, some people he regarded as friends ignored and rebuffed him. Others jeered, sneered, and even spat at him. Was he to blame for their loss of business? They obviously thought so. In fact, it seemed the entire village held him responsible for the whole sorry mess. Income was severely reduced, and people made no secret of the fact they felt deceived and humiliated. Apart from memorial stones, Lewis's main income was now from his work at Harewood House. Perhaps it was time for him to leave and move nearer Harrogate and Mel.

"And now to Whetherwell," Mel put her iron down to concentrate on the television.

"We have a report on how investigations into the weeping Madonna are affecting the villagers."

She saw Lewis come from his house and snap at a journalist.

"I've lost my wife and my child. Now I'm being driven from my home. I wish to be left alone."

At that, he slammed his door in the cameraman's face. Her heart ached for him. She felt responsible for his unhappiness, at least in part, and wondered what she could do to ease his pain. The report then turned to Father McNally, who declared there would be an open meeting in the church.

"To try and settle the unrest," he said.

Hearing this, Mel knew what she must do.

The lighting in the church did little to improve the mood of the people as they trooped in, with umbrellas and waterproofs, to air their grievances.

"I always maintained there was nothing miraculous about the statue," said Lewis. "Didn't I fashion the stone myself, with my own hands?"

Several people accused him of spreading the rumours of miracles.

"A ruse to increase his profits," complained others.

"I said nothing about miracles," Lewis retorted.

"Yes, you did," a few more people added.

Father McNally was having difficulty keeping control. As complaints and accusations were fired from all quarters,

"It was me," uttered a lone voice.

Silence fell like a mist across the moors, and people turned to look at a woman with a small boy at the back of the church.

"I spoke about a miracle."

She told of her son's life-saving operation and what the surgeon had said.

"The medical staff did a remarkable job, but I wonder if I hadn't come here in desperation, would it have been so successful? What are the chances of a cavity in the statue's head and of the crack occurring where it did? What is the probability of these events taking place just before my son's operation? I am no churchgoer, and I seldom pray, but with these coincidences and my son alive and well, call it what you like; to me, it is a miracle."

Barely a whisper passed through the people gathered in the church. At length, Father McNally spoke and thanked Mel for sharing her story.

"You've taught us a lot," he said. "And given us all food for thought."

Hands were quietly extended, others murmured apologies, and real tears were shed that night in reconciliation.

The Dewhurst family was well represented at the meeting, and one of them suggested bringing the statue into the church. There was a general consensus of approval, and Lewis was pleased to clean and repair it, but he left the crack across her eyes for all to see. Finally, it was reverently placed upon a special stand where people could see it on their way in and out. A noticeboard was set up to accompany it, bearing newspaper articles and photographs explaining the truth behind the reports, along with an account from the museum about the discovery of the original statue.

Under the gaze of the Madonna of Wetherwell. Lewis and Mel became Mr and Mrs Phinn the following spring.

These days, they sell local craft items to tourists and those that visit from time to time to see what the frenzy had been about.

Michael is becoming a broad-shouldered lad, and he now has a nine-year-old half-brother, Ian. They enjoy helping with the sheep, taking them to pasture in the Yorkshire Dales and assisting at shearing time. More often, though, the boys are to be found in Lewis's workshop, learning from him the skills of his craft, such as those needed for the building and repair of dry stone walls; carving in stone and wood, finials, corbels, memorials, and of course figurines.

Their family and the gift shop with its little café keep Mel and Lewis very busy, and though he never forgot his first wife, the once lonely, grieving stone mason is now happy and content. Grateful for this second chance, he cannot believe such healing can all be down to luck. The family business looks secure, and his thoughts often return to the face he had glimpsed in that rough chunk of rock.

THE CROSSING

You ask me about the crossing. Was I there? What was it like?

How can I forget it? Indeed, such a momentous event should never be forgotten.

I was seventeen at the time, yet I can recall it as vividly as if it were yesterday, even after sixty years.

Since escaping from Egypt, we had trekked through the wilderness, led by our God, in a pillar of cloud by day and one of fire by night. This allowed us to make as much headway as possible without stopping. Exhausted, we pitched camp near a place called Pi-hahiroth. There, our flocks and herds fed hungrily on the scant desert pasture while we refreshed ourselves with what little food we had.

As evening drew in, rumours began to spread around the camp that Pharaoh's army was only a short distance away in pursuit of us. People began to fear the awful fury they would wreak upon us. Soon, in the twilight, rank upon rank of horsemen and chariots appeared on the horizon. We were hemmed in by high mountains, and the Sea of Reeds (sometimes known as the Red Sea), with no way out. The Egyptians were about to close in on us.

People were angry and afraid. I can remember my stomach churning as I brooded on the prospect of us being cut down like so much herbage. Many said they wished they had never left Egypt even though our masters had treated us worse than dogs.

"Are there no graves in Egypt?" asked others, "that you have to bring us here to die?"

Some told Moses they knew this would happen and asked why he hadn't listened. In an effort to bring order, Moses held up his hand and reminded us of what the Lord had done in Egypt. He told us all not to be afraid as Yahweh was about to bring us victory. I was angry myself. Was that all he could say? – Was it empty rhetoric to placate us? My heart was pounding as we packed up our tents and belongings. My mother, always the strong one in our family, tried to keep us busy to take our minds off the impending blood bath.

"Hod," she called to my father, "don't sit there with your head in your hands, lamenting your fate. You're a disgrace to the tribe of Asher. Go and help Jotham with the oxen."

So we both yoked them, ready to move on, but where? Yes, I was scared, but I wasn't going down without a fight. We had farm implements that would double as weapons, as well as swords that we had plundered from our overlords. If we were to die, I was determined to take as many Egyptians with me as I could.

We all stood together, ready to face our foe, when, quite unexpectedly, the situation changed. The pillar of cloud we had been following suddenly moved to our rear, between our enemies and us. The cloud darkened in the failing light until it became like dense smoke. Its mantle completely disoriented our pursuers so they could no longer reach us. Fire flashed from its core, lighting up the sea a short distance before us.

"Forward!" commanded Moses.

Were we to go into the sea? That was the direction in which we were advancing, and I wondered if he had some desperate death wish that we should drown rather than being taken by Pharaoh's army. So, forward we went to the very shore. Here, Moses lifted his staff, the one with which, many said, he had worked miracles. Then stretched out his hand over the sea. At once, a strong easterly wind arose, increasing in such force and intensity we feared we would be blown into the waves. At that point, a rift appeared in the sea straight out into the night.

"March on!" came the cry.

People hesitated, and like many others, I looked back to see if there was another way, but the angel of Yahweh was driving us, and into this void we had to go; with fire from the pillar of cloud lighting our way in the darkness.

The water stood up on either side of us, higher than a temple, making a terrifying rumbling, crashing sound. The ground was rocky with stretches of caked mud, but our mules were sure-footed, and with some persuasion, the large, thick, solid wheels on our wagons enabled us to negotiate the terrain. On and on, we went through that endless night, trudging, slipping, pushing, while all the time, the strong wind kept back the terrifying waters that we feared would engulf us. As if all this wasn't enough, although we couldn't see them, we knew the Egyptians were following.

The crossing lasted an eternity as we toiled through the endless night. At last, I heard a cry.

"Land ahead!"

Was it true? Yes. The shore was in sight. With what strength remained, the long convoy of all the tribes of Israel struggled with their belongings onto the bank; the weaker ones were aided by the strong, while others persuaded the animals to climb ashore.

All my family were accounted for except my sister. In the confusion of livestock and people coming ashore, she was not to be seen. Then I saw her still some way back in the channel, barely able to go another step, and Moses was about to lift his hand over the water.

"Stop, stop," I yelled desperately and dashed back into the sea.

"Jotham, Jotham, no! It's too late! Not you as well," wailed my mother in anguish.

But with a strength that wasn't mine, I reached my sister and carried her to safety.

Far off down in the abyss between those walls of water lit by the fiery pillar, we could see the vanguard of the Egyptians straining to advance; their thoroughbred horses and finely wrought chariots were becoming hopelessly stuck in the mud. Certain now there were no more of us to come, Moses stretched his hand out over the sea. At once, the wind abated, and the water flowed back to its place. There was no escape for Pharaoh's army. They were too far from land, and fearful whirlpools dragged them into the depths.

So, my friend, you can tell the next generation how it was from one who lived through it. For the first time, we were a free nation, and as the sun rose, it revealed the bodies and chariots of our enemy littering the banks. With grateful hearts, we raised a hymn of praise to our great God, who had delivered us all with such terrible, all-powerful love.

THE LEGACY

"As poor as a church mouse, goes the old saying," said the storyteller as she settled down to tell her children the family legend that had been passed down to her through many generations.

"Now, here is how it all began. Your ancestor, Marietta, lived in a crack between the foundation stones of a ruined wayside chapel. She didn't consider herself any poorer than her neighbours who lived outside, in the fields; in fact, she thought she was lucky to have such shelter.

No one ever visited. The place was derelict, so she was quite surprised when a youth came and spent a long time there, just kneeling amongst the debris and gazing at a large picture of a man with outstretched arms, which had hung there for as long as she could remember. Eventually, he left, and she did not expect to see him again, but several days later, he returned dressed in tattered, worn clothes and began fixing one stone upon another. Could it be that he was attempting to rebuild the church? This was worrying. Would she lose her access to the surrounding fields, or worse still, her home? The man sat down on a pile of stone. He looked weary as he began to eat a small loaf of bread. Marietta looked out anxiously from her crack in the masonry, trying to remain unseen, but the man's sharp eyes caught sight of her, and she felt transfixed by them.

'Don't worry, little sister," he said. "Your home will be safe,' and he threw her a scrap from his meal, which she felt he could ill afford.

Day in, day out, disregarding the weather, the young man kept laying one brick after another. So slow and painstaking was the work; it didn't look like he would ever finish it; until another man joined him, then, later on, several more. They worked hard, night and day, and the church was eventually finished, with a new roof and windows. Poor folk from the nearby town came to sing and give thanks. What joy there was! Marietta also gave thanks because the good men were careful to make sure she had all she needed and that she could come and go as she pleased.

In time, the men left the little church, and it became the home of some poor ladies. They wore plain rough clothes, as the men did, and lived the same simple life, joyfully helping other people, except they never went beyond the walls and lived on what the townsfolk provided. Much as they do now," Pepe's mother explained.

Her children never tired of hearing the story, but this time something was different.

"There is a man close by," she said. "He is lying on a straw bed in the shadows because even though he is blind, the light hurts his eyes. He is weak, and the poor ladies wash and tend wounds on his hands, feet, and side. He must be very special, and I am wondering who he is."

Pepe peeped out from a crack in the wall, across a dimly lit, bare stone floor to a figure lying on a pile of straw. The man was struggling to sit up while one of the ladies gave him some broth with a small piece of bread. Pepe's cousins were running around and over this gentle man while he threw them crumbs from his meal.

"Pepe, come back," said his mother." You may watch, but I don't want you bothering him like so many of our relatives are doing."

Pepe gazed at him. He was very thin and wan, clothed in tattered rags with a rough piece of cord around his waist. His wounds looked very painful, but he didn't seem to complain; instead, his lips were moving as if he was trying to work something out in his mind. Pepe couldn't take his eyes off him. There was something so attractive and compelling about him. He watched for a long time, inching his way forward, just to be near him.

When the broth was finished, one of the poor ladies came in to take the bowl.

"Sister Clare," whispered the man.

"Peace, Brother Francis," she said.

Then the man lifted up his voice and sang joyfully. He sang of Brother Sun, Sister Moon, Brothers Wind and Air, Sister Water, Brother Fire, and Sister Mother Earth. He sang of all creation calling everything his brothers and sisters. Even Death was his sister, and he did not fear her embrace. Creeping closer to him, Pepe touched his hand. He thought he hadn't been noticed, particularly with all the other mice running around, but he was wrong.

Slowly the man lifted his hand, and Pepe could see the deep scar on it. He held his hand over the little mouse, who froze in its shadow.

"God bless you, brother mouse," he murmured.

A warm glow spread throughout Pepe's body, and although nothing seemed to have changed, he knew he'd been given something very special.

Romance

FEVER OR FOREVER

When storms flash and rumble around the Mawddach hills; when the mountains are hidden in the cloud; then a giant is smelting gold, so folklore says, and it runs into the river down to the sea.

Gareth closed his laptop. Interesting as these folk tales were, they didn't help in researching his Great Uncle Selwyn. He felt, as a beneficiary in his Great Uncle's will, he should know something about the old man before meeting the solicitor. All he could glean from his parents and relatives was that his Great Uncle had lived in the Snowdonia district, but he could discover little else owing to some ancestral dispute. So the internet seemed the best alternative.

"He must have taken a shine to you," said the solicitor.

He handed Gareth some keys along with the deeds of a substantial holding.

"Nobody else in your family has received anything from him. Oh, you're to have this also."

Slowly, Gareth opened a small envelope and read the note.

Dear Gareth,
When you get this letter, my ashes will have been scattered to the four winds over the Mawddach estuary. I doubt if you remember meeting me, but in your infant face and gestures, I detected many of my own traits, which is why I have chosen to bequeath to you my home.

If you keep level-headed, this could be a golden opportunity for you.

Wishing you success in your life's journey.
Your Great Uncle Selwyn.

Gareth knew there was gold in Snowdonia. It had been used by royalty for generations, but what had it to do with this property he'd inherited?

"What did the solicitor say, Gary?"

He had been roused from his reverie by his partner Cathy, an attractive brunette whose looks belied a tender astuteness.

"Perhaps things are looking up, Cath."

He showed her the deeds.

"Our mortgage problems may soon be over, courtesy of Great Uncle Selwyn. Perhaps we could look through them tonight."

Together they pored over the documents of an estate comprising several buildings.

"It covers quite a sizeable area, Cath. Apart from the house, there's a row of barrack-type dwellings."

"Self-contained living quarters? What great holiday accommodation!"

"Given a good make-over, yes, and there's lovely countryside around."

They discussed the possibilities at some length until the clock chimed in the lounge.

"Gary, it's getting late. I'll make some coffee."

No sooner had she gone than Gareth called her back excitedly.

"Look, Cath. This paragraph, here. There's a gold mine in the grounds. Just a stone's throw from the house. A real gold mine. How awesome is that? It must be what the old boy meant."

"Steady on, Gary. Look further down. See? It's been blocked up since 1899. It's all mined out."

"Just my luck. At least we can check this place out. With sleeping bags and supplies, we could bunk down for a weekend."

"Why not go this Friday?" suggested Cathy. "I'm sure someone will do my shift at the hotel. What about you?"

"I've no major joinery jobs until next week."

Rain drizzled from the trees as they drove up a narrow pass through the Coed y Brenin forest. Their satnav directed them to an unmade driveway.

"We may as well go with it, Cath. We're lost otherwise."

"Gary, Gary, there it is."

As the car lurched around a bend, the house came into sight, and they were soon looking out over a mist-shrouded valley.

"The view must be stunning on a fine day," Cathy exclaimed.

Gareth agreed, but his mind was on something else.

"First thing tomorrow, I'm going to look for that gold mine."

"Is that all you can think of? What about the potential of this place as a holiday residence? Isn't that more important? And it's not beyond our capabilities."

The place had real prospects, so they decided to take a risk and soon moved to their new home, Barn Mynydd (Mountain View).

They lived simply and frugally, putting all their resources to work on building their dream. They both spent long hours designing, renovating and decorating. Gareth, however, was drawn to studying the information on Welsh gold mining that he had previously downloaded from the internet. The prospect of making a strike preyed on his mind night and day until he felt compelled to swing a pick-axe at the mine entrance.

A dark, damp passageway opened into the mountain. Cautiously he entered. Highlighted in the beam of his torch, rough shale littered the floor while occasional chunks of hard greyish green rock glistened in the wet, crumbly mudstone walls, indicating the possibility of a gold-bearing quartz seam.

"Gary, you're filthy!" said Cathy. "Where have you been?"

"Just exploring."

"You've opened that mine haven't you? You can't leave it alone. Don't you realise how dangerous it is? I need your help here."

To Gareth, the mine was like a drug. There must still be gold in there, and he was going to find it regardless of Cathy's remonstrations.

He hewed away the soft substrate in various places until, glinting in the beam from his helmet light, he found a solid layer of quartz. The rock was resistant and the progress slow, yielding barely a bucket of chippings for an hour's work.

"There you are, Gary!"

Cathy found him in one of the outbuildings breaking rocks and examining the fragments.

"I thought you were busy putting up shelves, and now I find you here. What's the matter with you? Are you losing interest in our project or something? You are completely obsessed with this gold business. You have no experience, and that makes it doubly dangerous," she continued, anxious and exasperated. "Ask yourself if it's worth the risk. I'm busy in chalet three if you need me."

Glumly, Gareth continued searching the quartz. What was that? Something caught his eye. He looked closer. Yes, there, in a flake of stone, shimmered a minute vein of what could only be gold. Now, what would she say to this?

"I'm not interested, Gary. We're supposed to be preparing holiday accommodation, and you are wasting time on this futile pursuit."

"Futile, is it? We'll see how futile it is when I've more than enough gold to pay off our debts."

With this, Gareth stormed out into the rain.

He attacked the walls of the mine with mounting zeal ignoring the rainwater dripping down his neck from fissures in the roof. A sharp grating sound, however, made him pause. Crack – it reverberated again. There was no time to lose getting out. He grabbed his bucket of rocks and struggled as quickly as he could towards the exit. Rubble bombarded him, knocking and disabling the torch from his builder's helmet while the daylight at the end of the tunnel abruptly disappeared. The darkness pitched him headlong into a panic. Desperately, he attempted to dig his way to freedom. The air was becoming increasingly foetid; his fingers were raw down to the nail-beds. He remembered his mobile phone and switched it on, but there was no signal. Its light swam before his eyes while he entered another realm.

Rumbling cracking sounds are heard as a colossal, indistinct figure broods over a huge fiery clay furnace, boosted by a large pair of bellows. A bright rivulet of molten metal trickles down the mountainside.

A man's voice cries, "Stop! That's precious gold you're wasting."

"I'm the Guardian of the Mawddach estuary, Gareth. This gold spreads through the whole river – right down to the sea. It gives life to the valley. Soon, you'll see it." The shadowy figure pumps the bellows furiously and is soon lost in clouds of smoke.

"What do you mean? How will...? How?"

"Gary, Gary," said a familiar voice. You're OK; you're safe now. Thank God you're back."

"Cathy? Where am I?"

218

"You're in an ambulance on the way to the hospital in Aberystwyth. I guessed something had happened to you in that mine. The firemen and mountain rescue people dug you out."

She choked back tears of stress and relief.

"Don't you ever leave me like that again? You could have been killed!"

Tests and scans complete; Gareth was finally discharged. He sat quietly while Cathy drove home, back to Barn Mynydd, as glowering clouds threatened more rain.

"Gary, what's wrong? You've hardly spoken a word since we left the hospital."

"I've been a fool, Cath. I'm afraid we may not be ready for the holiday season. I've wrecked our dreams?"

"No, Gary, love, you haven't. There's still time, but remember, the consultant said to take it easy for a while. I thought gold fever only happened in films, until now."

The weather remained changeable, but the forecasts promised an improvement.

"Cathy, come quick," Gareth called one evening.

There was an urgency in his voice. She'd told him not to overdo it, but he wouldn't listen and had spent every waking hour preparing for their first influx of visitors, due in a few weeks. He seemed to be calling from the terrace, and she hurried out, hoping it was nothing too serious.

"Look!"

He pointed across the estuary, gleaming in the intense amber light of the setting sun.

"The river, the sea!"

Cathy gazed at him perplexed, fearful the mine incident had affected his brain. Since leaving the hospital, Gareth had spoken more than once about some vision he'd had while trapped in the tunnel.

"There's the gold. Spilling down the hillside, just as I was promised. We can share it with all our guests. They will come here to experience and enjoy the beauty of this land. Now I know what Great Uncle Selwyn was hinting at."

Spontaneously, in a moment of rapture, Gareth knelt on one knee.

"Cathy, will you marry me?"

MARKET VALUES

A youth, dressed in shabby britches, waistcoat, and cap, waits in the shadow of the east gate of an old walled market town. A carter emerges on his way to collect produce from surrounding farms.

"Hey, Mr Jones, have you any messages for me today?"

The horse slows to a halt. "Yes, Alfie, she handed me one for you this morning, but mark my words; this will all end in tears."

The boy takes the note, and the carter continues over a time-worn bridge spanning a meandering river.

Alfie belonged to a company of travellers who toured the district, setting up their rag-tag collection of stalls and booths every Friday outside the town walls to sell everything from ostentatious lampstands to household utensils, toys, and rat traps. Unusually for a lad of his status in Victorian England, Alfie could read, thanks to his grandmother, who had been an actress. He leans against a buttress and scans the crumpled piece of paper.

Dear Alfie.

Things are getting difficult at home. My father keeps asking me if I am seeing that 'wretched tinker', as he calls you. I can't keep avoiding the question. He disapproves of you because you are from the outer market. He watches my every move. So, my love, I cannot meet you tonight. Don't be downcast. I will try to think of something and send another note next Friday at the usual time.

Loving you always.
Elsie

He sits staring into the river and recalls how they'd met.

*   *   *

Leaving town one evening, he heard a sharp cry. A vixen? No, he knew that one. He pressed himself into the shadow of a tree and saw two shapes attacking the figure of a girl. Feeling for her plight, he had gone to her aid, fists flying on wiry arms used to fighting for survival. However, the girl, seeing she had an ally, had set to with all her energy until the ruffians were successfully vanquished.

"You fight good for a girl. Did they take anything?"

"Some money my Dad give me for Fanny's services last night."

"Oh, the prostitute that lives by the bridge. What will you do?"

The girl shrugged. "Dunno. Go home, I s'pose. Thanks for your help."

Alfie offered his hand.

"Can I see you to your door?"

"No, no, you don't know my Dad."

"I'm not afraid. My name's Alfie. Where do you live?"

"Brewery Lane, near the market hall. Name's Elsie. My Dad owns a drapers business there."

In the narrow street, she lifted a large brass knocker on a dark heavy door with trembling hands. A grim-faced, burly man peered out.

"Where've you been? Who's this?"

"Dad, I've had trouble. He helped me."

Disregarding her protests, Elsie's father dragged her inside and slammed the door. Alfie could hear shouts and screams from inside. He hammered on the door, which was opened a few minutes later by the same man brandishing a cane.

"What's goin' on?" said Alfie. "Don't you hurt her."

"None of your business. Get out, go on."

Alfie put his foot in the door. He flinched as the stick bit his legs and retreated as Elsie's father lashed out at him.

Under one of the bridge's arches, the lad examined his wounds. He liked Elsie. She had more spunk in her than some of his mates. The carter approached the town gate on his evening deliveries.

"Mr Jones, wait on. Can you do me a favour and take a message to the draper's daughter in the market."

"Elsie, I know her. I'll see what I can do. Hurry now, or I'll be late."

Alfie scribbled with a pencil stub on an old price ticket.

You're a fine girl Elsie. Meet me tomorrow evening at St. Hilda's niche. Your Alfie.

Near a hollow within the walls where a patron saint once stood, he paced uncertainly. No longer frequented by devotees, this was now a secluded place, away from prying eyes. He waited until the moon was well up. She wouldn't come now. He may as well go. Slowly he headed for the gate.

"Alfie," said a low breathless voice. "I thought you might have gone. Unfortunately, I couldn't get away any earlier."

Here, every Friday, they met to embrace, kiss, and talk of love.

"Will you come away with me, Elsie? My folks would like to see yer."

"I dunno, Alfie. Would they really want to meet a toffee-nosed girl from the market hall?"

"You're not like that, Elsie."

"I'm afraid Dad will find us and kill you."

Saturday mornings, for another interminable week, Alfie was obliged to leave early with the other travellers for the next town.

"This is just an infatuation," said Alfie's father. "We need you to help pitch and strike the stall, sell stuff, not to mention look after the horse."

"But she needs me, and I need to be with her."

"I'll hear no more, Alfie, You will come with us, and that's final."

*   *   *

Elsie's note is worrying. What could her father be doing to her? Knowing how to keep a low profile, Alfie makes for the market hall to look for her. He is about to enter the town when a shrill whistle sounds behind him, followed by a clamorous horn blown by a man in a red uniform. Looking around, he sees a large red truck spewing steam, carrying a large pump affair, and drawn by two galloping cart horses carrying a crew in similar uniforms. It comes from the direction of the river. Alfie steps quickly aside as the fire engine hurtles through the gate. He follows, his nostrils tingling. It is soon evident that the market hall must be on fire. Victims are being dragged out. He recognises one burly body in particular. Elsie, she's in there. Flames billow from the doors and windows. He must find her. Her stall? Falling timber further confuses the bewildering array of aisles, arcades, and galleries. The almost appetising aroma of roasting meat from the flesher's stall is quickly replaced by the acrid stench of charring carrion. Coughing in spasms, he holds his kerchief over his nose and comes across a draper's stall.

"Elsie! Elsie!"

Bolts of smouldering cloth lie in scattered heaps issuing thick choking fumes.

With a sickening creak, a beam comes crashing from the roof, pinning him to the floor. The heat is intense, his senses blurred.

"Alfie! Alfie! Come on, get up."

Elsie stands before him like some vision of a guardian angel. He struggles but can't get free. She grabs a bar, thrusts it under the beam and pushes it up with her whole weight. Ignoring the pain, Alfie wriggles free. He tries to stand. Falls.

"Go, Elsie, go. I'll manage."

"I'm not leaving you, Alfie. Here lean on my shoulder."

She heaves him up, her shoulder under his arm. Choking and spluttering, they stumble and stagger down the nearest aisle. Molten wax spills from a candlemaker's stall and flares up in front of them, preventing any advance, while fallen girders bar their return.

"Quick, Alfie, down here. I know this way. It's our only chance."

They lurch down stone steps into a cellar-like vault. Some small high-level windows admit a dim light from the street above. A draught blows down the corridor.

"It's less smoky here," said Elsie. "There are several of these basement passages. Dad says they were made to provide fresh air for the market."

"Elsie, your dad...."

"I know Alfie. He was trying to save his stock."

226

Turning a corner, daylight from a grill at the end of the passage highlights a stack of barrels.

"Illicit brandy. They bring it in through that grill," Elsie remarks.

"Elsie. I can smell alcohol from the kegs. It'll draw the fire down here. You go ahead."

"No, we'll make it together, Alfie, or not at all. Here, get in this hand cart."

She rushes with him down the passageway and pulls free the grating from a window above a wooden ladder.

"I can't do it, Elsie; I'll never make it."

"Of course, you can. Com'on. Take my hand. No, hold the ladder, and I'll push you."

Fire rolls rapidly along the ceiling. A barrel explodes, filling the passage with blue flames. Spirit floods out along the corridor from others, adding to the inferno; its intense heat causing the ceiling to crack and collapse.

*   *   *

Carts, vardos, and covered wagons are beginning to cross the bridge. The travellers are leaving for the next town. A woman with a weather-beaten face but still bearing the evidence of beauty sits inside one of them. She soaks a cloth in a herbal mixture murmuring.

"Neither of you would ha' got out alive If there'd ha' been no help to hand."

TWO'S COMPANY

It's time they went. It really is. Oh, dear! I'm beginning to sound like my Mum. I remember the day she said to us, "It's time you left home and made your own way in the world."

So we did. We were all very excited at the prospect and a bit naive. I'll never forget the dreadful night when my brothers came knocking at my door. Their houses had been blown down, and they had escaped within a whisker of their lives. Well, that was over three years ago now, and they've been living with me ever since. I only built my house big enough for one person, and that's me, so there's no way all three of us can live in it. They still seem considerably traumatised by their experience, and though, at the time, we disposed of the 'lurking terror' as they called it, they are still afraid to go further than the garden gate. Mind you, my house was threatened too, but luckily it stood up to the onslaught. I had built it with a job-lot of bricks I got from a local builder, and I'm now working hard in a call centre to pay for them.

I wish my brothers would get some sort of employment. Extra money coming in would be a great help, but jobs are hard to come by these days. I'm sure counselling would go a long way in building up their confidence so that they can face the world again. They do a few chores around the house, but sometimes I think they may be taking advantage of me.

I wish I had the room to invite my girlfriend for a few nights. She really is very alluring, with attractive eyes that look at you in such a loving way and a big friendly smile. I met her when I went to see The Jungle Book at our local 'flea-pit'. It was love at first sight. She kissed me with such passion that I invited her to have a meal with me at a local Merry Grill. Here she wolfed down nearly a dozen burgers before I was even halfway through the one I had. I must admit I was a bit shocked, but she has such an endearing personality. Several people say she is too hairy and try to warn me against her, but they don't know her like I do. I explained to her the problem I was having at home. She was very understanding and assured me that it would not be long before my brothers were gone, but I don't know how she could be so sure.

One of my brothers is not very bright when it comes to practical matters. He has no idea of how to cope with the real world. He made his home out of a pile of straw he found in a field, so I'm not surprised it blew down. My other brother is quite good at joinery. He can make all sorts of things out of wood, and he built his house with some old packing crates he had bought at a reduced rate over the internet. It looked very cosy, but he hadn't laid any foundations, so of course, that blew down too.

My girlfriend says she is really looking forward to meeting them when she comes for tea tonight. I'm very excited. I hope she will like them.

Glimpses

THE DRAWER

He pushed it, he pulled it, he turned the knob this way and that, but the drawer wouldn't budge.

"Is it one of those dummy drawers?" said his partner. You know, like you get in front of the kitchen sink."

"Julie, this isn't under the kitchen sink, is it? It's under the bench on the other side of the room."

"Well, perhaps it should have been under the sink or something. Harry, do come away. Leave it alone. We're supposed to be having a quiet night in together."

Harry joined Julie in the meal she presented, a tempting array of all his favourite appetisers. However, even as they enjoyed these snacks and the film together, the drawer was still, annoyingly, on his mind.

He'd looked in the cupboard underneath, and a compartment definitely existed. Unfortunately, there was no obvious keyhole or lock, so he concluded that it must be glued shut for some reason. One way or another, however, he was going to open it; with a chisel if necessary. What was the point of having a drawer if you couldn't use it?

The flats seemed to have been thrown up in no more than a week. Their prices being rock bottom, Julie and Harry could just about afford the mortgage. In the first couple of days after moving into their new apartment, they were still checking out its less obvious features when they discovered that one of the kitchen drawers would not open.

The following morning, Harry took a chisel and hammer and managed, at least, to prise off the drawer front, but, even more perplexing, the compartment was blocked by a blank piece of chipboard. He gave it a push, and the sealed compartment moved back under the bench, leaving the cupboard space an extra six inches higher. He showed it to his partner.

"What sort of a drawer is this? It goes right into the wall, but I can't get into it?"

"At least we've got room to store the stools. I don't think they're too tall."

Julie stacked the seats that accompanied their small kitchen table, and they fitted as she had said. Now, although the procedure of swinging a cat would still be rather difficult, there was at least a bit more space for more routine activities.

That evening, while watching television, Julie and Harry were startled to hear a loud bang.

"Intruders!" Julie sounded fearful.

"How can anybody possibly get in here? We're on the fourth floor. If they didn't come in through our front door, they'd need an unusually long ladder."

"What can it be then?" asked Julie. "I suppose a bird might get in if we'd left the kitchen window open, but we haven't."

Harry grabbed a letter opener, the only thing they had in the lounge that might serve as a weapon.

"Harry, do be careful. It could be anyone, anything."

"I can't just sit quaking in my boots. You stay here, Julie."

"No way, I'm coming with you."

They both crept out of the lounge.

"Hush," whispered Harry as Julie began to giggle. "That's no help at all."

Cautiously, they entered the kitchen and were dismayed by what they saw. The door of the cupboard under the bench was wide open, and the stools had fallen out.

"Pushed out," said Harry as he showed Julie that the sealed drawer had come right forward again. Then, completely bewildered, Harry pushed it back.

"I'll have to sort this out tomorrow."

About half an hour into their favourite soap opera, the strange phenomenon occurred again. Harry pushed the thing back.

"There's nothing we can do now except watch what happens."

Harry and Julie settled on their stools and prepared for a lengthy vigil, but no more than ten minutes later, the sealed drawer came forward again.

"It must be on some sort of spring," said Harry.

He pushed it back, and within a few minutes, the strange, sealed drawer shot forward once more.

"What can be the purpose of that?" said Julie.

"Who knows? It's completely useless. I suggest we replace the bench when we can afford it."

This time he pushed it back as hard as he could, and the thing disappeared altogether. Instead, there was a crash behind the bench. He was about to speak when a voice took the words right out of his mouth.

"I've never seen anything so stupid! I'll have to get to the bottom of this."

There were sounds of movement behind the workbench. Harry bent down to see what was going on and almost fell backwards as he saw another face looking back at him.

"What do you think you're doing?" it said. "I'm Ted Barnes, your neighbour, and you have just upset my cutlery drawer."

DÉJÀ VU

Hunched under his coat, its collar turned up against the weather, a man walks home through thin sodium-stained smog. Suddenly, from a dark alley, a hand strikes out, silencing his cries, and a body is thrust into a car which makes off towards the river. An outboard motor splutters into life and through the gloom slips a boat from which a man heaves a heavy bundle, received by the water with a gurgle.

"What a way to go! I suppose he'll be missed."

"He did ask for it, John. Anyway, he's gone now, to pastures new, so to speak."

"I know your wife liked him, didn't she?"

"Oh yes, Max. Jean has even got his autograph, but I didn't care for him. Too much of a charmer. You felt you couldn't trust him. Do you know if he'll come back or be replaced in some way?"

The satisfied director chuckled.

"I doubt it. You never know, though; the guys on the panel play their cards pretty close to their chests. They're discussing a new storyline next Tuesday. Your work is good, so we'll need you there."

Max stood up, stretched, smoothing his greying hair as the credits rolled, "It's getting late. Your good wife will be expecting you."

"Yeah, I'd better ring and tell her I'm on my way."

John Blake tapped his phone, and waited for an answer, then returned it to his pocket.

"No reply. She's often late. Busy organising some function with her art group, I expect; goodness knows what they have to talk about."

John entered his empty home, dim lighting accentuating his gaunt appearance. He made his own supper and flicked on the television—the same old news. A clip of West Beginners caught his attention. Normally he didn't watch his own work after Max had passed the filming, but this was a report on one of the actors. Unremitting; however, he began to work on another episode.

"Hi, John, I'm home," Jean called cheerily. The lounge smelled of toasted cheese. She bent down and gave him a peck on the cheek; she smelt of Parisienne, the perfume he gave her last Christmas.

"Hard at work, dear?"

"I've got a deadline to meet."

"Not more cutbacks, I hope?"

"No, Paul's the last one, at least for now. "

Jean laughed nervously.

"I believe he's going to advertise chewing gum in California?"

The doorbell rang. Two men in uniform enquired if her husband was at home.

"John, the police want a word with you," called Jean, inviting them in from the chilly, damp night.

"Just a formality, Mr Blake, said an officer. Would you mind telling us where you were between eight and ten o'clock this evening?"

"Why, I was here, writing. Anything wrong?"

"A body has been found in the river," he replied.

"Anyone I know?"

"Possibly; it's Paul Keaton, the West Beginners actor."

Jean gave a stifled gasp, flushed, and hastily left the room.

John grimaced. So, he was right; she had been having an affair with him.

THE TEA PARTY

The auctioneer, did he say The Tea Party? Yes, that's the painting. It takes me back to a golden summer's day when I was staying with my Grandmother, at her cottage, full of treasures, smells of baking, and furniture polish. It was always a treat to go there. We did such wonderful things together.

I'll never forget that day. Someone special was coming, and I was helping Grandma deadhead the roses in her beautiful garden

"Who's coming, Grandma?" I asked.

"Wait and see," she said.

But it's very hard for a little child like I was then to wait, even for five minutes.

At last, Grandma took off her pinafore, and we both set out along the lane to the village. First, we went to the butchers and the greengrocers. Next, we went to the bakers, where Grandma bought some fairy cakes. Lastly, in the post office, she asked for a quarter of dolly mixtures. Wide-eyed with anticipation, I watched the shopkeeper lift a large jar from the ranks of humbugs and barley sugar sticks. As he removed the lid, a delicious aroma filled my senses. I loved dolly mixtures. There were so many different kinds, fondant shapes and sugared jellies, with such lovely colours and subtle flavours. He tipped some into a big shiny pan on the scales, then poured them into a little paper bag holding the corners, and tossing it over, twisting them round to keep it closed.

It didn't stay closed for long, though.

"Alright," said Grandma. "You can have a couple now, but we must save the rest until we get home."

Back at the cottage, we laid a blue gingham-check table cloth on the grass among the fragrant flowers, with a beautiful doll-sized bone china tea set that Grandma had never let me play with before. I decorated the fairy cakes with some of the sweets, then shared the others out on the little plates among my favourite toys, several Teddies, Jumbo, Mickey the Monkey, Charlie the Clown and Betty the rag doll. Of course, I had to try some myself, to be sociable, you understand.

"Our guest is here," said Grandma from the French windows. "This is my friend Emil. He's going to paint you."

He set up his easel and painted while I played, asking me to pause occasionally while he concentrated on some detail. By bedtime, he had all but finished and showed me the picture you see here today on auction. Every detail is just as it was, even those little sweets painted with such care; they still make my mouth water. The picture may sell for thousands of pounds, but my memory of that perfect day is priceless.

I DON'T WANT A BATH

Itch, itch, scratch, scratch. This itch is driving me mad. It's driving my human mad too. He took me to the vet's; I hate it there. I get prodded, poked, and stuck with needles. I try to bite him, but my owner scolds me, and then I get muzzled. Thankfully, there wasn't much of that this time. I just sat on the table, all forlorn, while he examined me. He gave my human a large packet. Pills, I thought; I'll never get through all of them.

"Bath him three times daily for a week," the vet said, "and put two tablespoons of that powder in the water."

So that was it. I hate baths. They make me feel cold and miserable while people laugh at me. So here I am, out in the garden looking for somewhere to hide.

"Fido! Bath time."

That's my owner. Is he daft or what?

"Come on, Fido. It's not that bad. Nice, warm water. It'll make you feel better. Ha! There you are. I can see the tip of your tail."

Oh, that tail of mine, it always gives me away. I can see him coming with my collar and lead. That won't work; I know it's not walkies. I'll be dragged to a tub in the backyard, dumped in the water, and scrubbed. I won't complain, but I'll sit there and look so miserable the missus will take pity on me and give me a biscuit. Here he comes; here he comes, and here I go. Oh well, see you tomorrow by the birdbath.

THE TREE

Fearfully, I lay among the thousands of other acorns on the forest floor while a family of wild boars greedily scoffed the prized mast. I was relieved at being passed over, but soon after, I was grabbed by a couple of paws. It seemed I would be eaten after all. The squirrel, however, collecting nuts for its winter stores, buried me instead.

I soon germinated in the rich earth and grew into a sapling surrounded by tall trees reaching for the sunlight. I felt small and insignificant, dominated by these proud elders, but one day some men came to fell trees to build ships.

"Leave this little'n," said one. "It's not ready yet."

I now had light and space to flourish, increase my girth and stretch out broad limbs.

Today, I am over eight hundred years old, and stout wooden props support my tired, heavy boughs. Guides call me the King's Oak and tell of a time when an English monarch hid amongst my branches to escape his pursuers, but only I know the truth of this tale.

Now, I see a crowd around me protesting against a threat to clear my parkland to make way for a new superstore. Local people appreciate me, and I have loved them for centuries. Courting couples have carved their initials in my bark. Pensioners shelter in my shade. They value me for the tourists that visit, and I feel secure as long as I have my friends.

GONE FISHING

She stood on the busy quayside. The sea was sparkling, a beautiful blue in the bright sunshine. There was nothing to suggest there had been a storm the night before. The little boats gently bobbed on the water, and the gulls cried overhead. Some sounded mournful, and others seemed to be laughing. They sounded almost human at times.

Her husband had gone mackerel fishing with the crew of the Merry Maid, but he hadn't returned, and she feared the worst. Wreckage from the boat had been found washed ashore in the neighbouring bay. The bodies of several of the crew had been found further out to sea. No, he wasn't coming back.

Her eyes glazed over, and she seemed to be in another world. She turned and walked slowly home. She didn't hurry. The place would be empty, with the children at school. She felt numb and couldn't cry even though she wanted to. She put the key in her front door, which opened into the darkness of the hallway, and went through to the kitchen.

"Hello, Mira."

"Jack! Is it really you? Oh, thank God you're back."

Then the tears flowed.

"The boat was wrecked on Little Titan, and I managed to scramble ashore. I was picked up by the ketch Mary Rose this morning."

She gently tended his injuries sustained from the battering he had taken on the rocks. He was home. He was home.

SUNDAY LUNCH AT HUDSON CASTLE

Some friends, having recently moved to Rochdale, had invited me to Sunday lunch. Over sherry, Dan and Beryl told me about an invitation they'd received to Sunday lunch at a residence called Hudson Castle.

"I had never heard of the place," said Dan. "We'd only just moved and didn't know anyone, so I was sceptical as to whether this invitation was genuine."

"We had hoped to meet some interesting people there," added Beryl.

The satnav took them to Hudson Street, a cobbled backwater, and Hudson Castle, a small, terraced house. Miniature well-clipped hedges bounded a postage-stamp-sized patch of neatly manicured grass.

They were greeted by a couple wearing elegant clothes from another age. The guests were immediately struck by the large, eclectic collection of historical memorabilia, particularly an exquisite "Jacobean," said their hosts. "Sadly, it lacks a rook."

"What a coincidence," said Dan. "We've just bought a matching piece at a local flea market."

"It charmed us so," said Beryl.

They agreed to deliver it the following day but, upon arrival, found only derelict dwellings.

"We discovered that a seventeen-century fortification definitely existed once on the Hudson Street site," Dan explained.

"Unfortunately, our invitation is missing," said Beryl. "So we can't show it to you."

The little castle, however, still stands on their mantelpiece.

A LITTLE BIRD

Mrs Treadwell retrieved the newspaper her husband repulsed. A robot had replaced him since his retirement.

"All those years, all that training, and for what?" he complained.

An advertisement for volunteers in a local community project appealed to those with his very skills. She showed it to him; tried to encourage him, but he remained obstinate and morose.

"Thanks, Janet."

Mrs Treadwell replaced the receiver. She let her husband answer the next call. A long-standing friend rang needing help in a project benefitting the town's youth.

"Your expertise is vital. Will you meet us next Monday?"

Colin felt valued again. Yes, he would go and see what it was all about. First, he must tell his wife. Wouldn't she be surprised?

Printed in Great Britain
by Amazon

84785763R00142